Aaron's Leap

Aaron's Leap

Magdaléna Platzová

translated by
Craig Cravens

BELLEVUE LITERARY PRESS
NEW YORK

First Published in the United States in 2014 by
Bellevue Literary Press, New York

For Information Contact:
Bellevue Literary Press
NYU School of Medicine
550 First Avenue, OBV A612
New York, NY 10016

Library of Congress Cataloging-in-Publication Data
Platzová, Magdaléna, 1972–
 [Aaronuv skok. English]
 Aaron's leap / Magdalena Platzova; translated by Craig Cravens. — First
edition.
  p. cm.
 Includes bibliographical references and index.
 ISBN 978-1-934137-70-3 (pbk.)
 1. Jewish women artists—Czech Republic—Fiction. 2. Jewish children
in the Holocaust—Czech Republic—Terezín (Ústecký kraj)—Fiction. 3.
Holocaust, Jewish (1939–1945) Fiction.
I. Cravens, Craig Stephen, 1965– translator. II. Title.
 PG5040.26.L38A6213 2014
 891.8'636--dc23

2013035135

Bellevue Literary Press would like to thank all its generous
donors—individuals and foundations—for their support.

This publication is made possible by grants from:

▲ ▼▼ The National Endowment for the Arts
ART WORKS.

The New York State Council on the Arts with the support of
Governor Andrew Cuomo and the New York State Legislature
NYSCA

and Amazon.com

Book design and composition by Mulberry Tree Press, Inc.
Manufactured in the United States of America.

first edition

1 3 5 7 9 8 6 4 2

ISBN 978-1-934137-70-3

To the memory of three artists:
Friedl Dicker-Brandeisová
Anna Sládková
Zdenka Kriseová

An open window, where a sweet hope remained
All is so unsayable, Oh God, that it brings you
to your knees—astounded.

—Georg Trakl

Aaron's Leap

CHAPTER 1

Film People

SHE SITS ON THE FLOOR in front of her wardrobe, where she keeps her letters, photographs, diplomas, newspaper clippings, invitations, dried flowers, and faded tricolors, reminders of the founding of the republic, her First Communion, her graduation dance, the liberation, her wedding, the birth of her son, her parents' funeral, her son's wedding, the birth of her granddaughter, Milena, the Velvet Revolution, the first free elections, her exhibitions.

She goes through the letters, reads one after another, and sets some aside to be destroyed later. She considers how to do it. Burning them seems a bit overwrought, and she doesn't have a fireplace. But she can't just sling them in the trash because she can't bear the thought of them accidentally ending up on the top of the container or even in the filthy hallway. And whoever comes to empty the bin might see them. She doesn't have the strength to tear them up. Perhaps drown them like kittens and star-crossed lovers. Weigh them down with a stone, soak the paper—the ink will dissolve, liquefy, and become dirty river water flowing out to sea. She realizes she's still sentimental when face-to-face with her letters. That's why she's going to destroy them. And also so that whoever goes through her effects—if anyone finds it worthwhile—will see her precisely as

11

she wants to be seen: as a woman who simplified her life, freed herself from everything superfluous, and became an eye, pure and transparent, like her watercolors.

She also places aside a few of Berta's diaries. Her granddaughter, Milena, would like to read them when she gets the time.

She almost never has time. The old woman looks at her in the mornings and sees circles beneath her eyes, dissatisfaction; something's eating away at her, and therefore she runs around at night. In her, she sees her own anxieties from youth, her own ambitions, which will become hypertrophied and choked off by the banality of everyday life. She watches her granddaughter, smokes the first of her five daily cigarettes, and thinks about art. Kristýna Hládková, eighty-eight, is thinking about art. And about herself.

She's tired. She heaps the letters she hasn't yet gone through back into their boxes and locks them in the wardrobe.

A windstorm kicks up in the evening. Outside Prague, they say, it's become a hurricane. Kristýna sits on the couch opposite the window, staring out at the thin, rocking trunks of spruce and silver pines and the long branches of birch. The view from the window reminds her of a painting in which the flowing tresses of the birches merge with the loosened plaits of half-naked nymphs, forming arabesques that are forever the same. Even now she cannot stand Art Deco, with its mendacity and impurity, even now when her antipathy from youth might have grown dull beneath a layer of senescent nostalgia. She stands her ground and does not bemoan the stucco busts and flowers she battered from the walls of her apartment with her hammer. Her son held it against her. But how could anyone stand all that ornamentation? She who once upon a time blazed up for Kirche, Nolde, Marc Chagall, who was a revelation for her. Corbusier and Brâncuşi. The student of the artist K., in whose atelier she discovered Berta and, through her, another great love, Paul Klee.

Berta, my great friend and life's inspiration. That's what she'll say to the film people who came all the way from Israel to make a film about her.

Berta, she'll say, managed to breathe life into things. That's art. Reviving the dead, making us see things that we always pass over without giving them a second thought. She could wax enthusiastic over a segment of curtain just as much as a painting. I tended to disregard curtains.

On the other hand, this passion for everything around her pulled her away from her real work, or from what is generally considered real work. She left a few paintings behind. She treated her relationships just like her interiors—she sought to live her life truthfully, beyond all clichés, comfortable lies, self-delusions. Purity, honesty, freedom—that was the challenge of Berta's entire generation.

For that matter, I am not leaving behind anything more than a negligible personal trace myself. You don't have great talent, but it's beautiful, said my teacher, the painter K. It was all more complicated with Berta—she had great talent.

Whenever Kristýna discusses Berta, she has to discuss herself and vice versa.

Nevertheless, judged by the usual parameters, Kristýna was successful compared to Berta. After the regime change in 1989, she enjoyed several years of public interest: private exhibitions, awards, trips abroad. Journalists sought her out with questions about the recent past; they were surprised at the slights she had to endure. They shook their heads, and Kristýna felt split in two: Where had she been these forty years? Hadn't she been sitting in the same apartment all this time? And if she wasn't living on some absurd planet, where had all these people been living who were now showing up with their questions? A monograph on her had come out in the mid-nineties, and then interest in her died away just as quickly as it had arisen. Kristýna returned to her solitude and kept on working. She even assumed that during the last few years she could see more clearly and deeply than ever before. She experimented with grasses, tree bark, the surface of water; she drew so close to nature that it dissolved on the paper into mere intimations, casts, and cursory impressions. She'd had almost fifty more years than Berta and had ended where Berta had. She would never exceed her friend.

Judged by the usual parameters, Berta Altmann, whose name does not figure in any surveys of art history and who is known to only a few specialists on the Terezín ghetto, was not a great artist. By Kristýna's own yardstick, however, she was enormous. Berta dead, even today, provides Kristýna with more energy and enthusiasm than any of the sentient beings around her.

Kristýna stares at the swaying tree trunks and feels like she's in the mountains, in the damp, fresh air saturated with oxygen, on the forest slopes, which thrum like a four-lane highway. She summons up and recalls the feeling precisely. It's nighttime and someone, a young person, is trudging through the snow with a backpack toward a warm and cozy, obtainable goal that he keeps putting out of his mind, preferring that the trip in the wide-open and windy night last forever. She had titled one of her paintings *Open Path*. It showed a gleaming, mesh-encased, pulsating egg beneath a wide, vaulting sky.

The tiny figure toting a canvas backpack and trudging through the snow before her, stopping every now and then to marvel at the winter stars, is Berta. She misses her. Pain exhausts itself, but not emptiness.

I am standing at the window of my Prague apartment, looking out: down at the tracks and the little booth of the train station. My canvas is fastened to the easel. I paint. If they saw me at school, I'd be laughed at. They wouldn't believe their eyes. We used to burn easels! We never wanted to paint from life. We didn't want to lie. From the window! I am standing in my living room and painting what I see. I become the tracks, the train station, the reddish reflection on the roof of the building opposite. I wander. I cease to be that anxious, burdened woman. Like this, I feel calm, untroubled. I do not want to look within, but without.

Kristýna doesn't have to read Berta's diaries again. She knows them almost by heart.

Of course, Berta wrote them in German, even though during those eight years she had learned to speak Czech fairly well. She said she had Czech ancestors, like everyone from Vienna.

Kristýna turns out the lamp and sits in the dark. The city beyond the window shimmers and she can make out each branch, but inside the room the heavy gloom washes away the outlines of the furniture, and all that's left of the pictures are dark spots on the walls. Directly above Kristýna's head hangs a large panorama of Prague Castle, which she painted from the balcony of the painter K.'s studio, under his guidance. The river thrusts out from the canvas like a turgid tongue, with the rickety Charles Bridge slicing across it. The silhouette of the castle towers above the bridge, nervous and trembling, most likely from the reverberation of approaching German troops. On the opposite wall, above the piano, is Berta's bouquet of begonias: pastel colored flowers with delicate hairs illumined by the morning sun, stems submerged in clear water and glass. One of the sprays of flowers, Berta painted in the countryside—a moment of warmth, light, and tranquillity.

Kristýna drowses, still clothed, with an ashtray on the carpet next to the sofa. She used to drowse like this in front of her paintings when she didn't know how to continue. She would look at them for so long that the images would creep their way into her dreams. Just before waking, she would sometimes have a solution, usually something surprising and unexpected.

They arrived in the morning, precisely at ten o'clock. She had told them she didn't want to see anyone before ten.

They showed up in her room with lights, tripods, a camera, and a great number of cables. She offered them coffee and then decided to sit down, so she wouldn't trip over anything. She took a pencil and piece of paper lying on the table and started sketching: the director, the cameraman losing his temper because of the lighting, the script girl. The woman who'd sent them here was not with them.

A Czech Jew from Israel who appeared in Prague around five years ago started going through the archives and prying into everything concerning Berta. She said she herself painted as well as wrote, mostly about people murdered and forgotten. She had proclaimed herself the memory of mankind, Kristýna thought to herself when the woman showed up the first time. Besides, dead Jews are good business. She was immediately ashamed of this ugly thought, and to punish herself, she treated the woman more kindly than she had initially intended.

She is trying to banish her nervousness by drawing. Suddenly, she doesn't feel so good. What does she actually know about Berta? Who gave her the right to talk about her to a camera? And what if they ask her something personal? It's none of their business. But if we omit the personal, what's actually left of Berta?

She's already trapped; the soundman is attaching a microphone to the edge of her shirt.

She had promised to talk about her memories. And she'd known Berta only as a happily married woman. She knew nothing about her earlier life. Well, she actually did; it was in her diaries. But she wasn't going to show them her diaries.

Perhaps she could say that Berta had longed for a child. And never had one.

They offered to take Milena with them. To Terezín and Hronov, where Berta had lived the last few years, before she was deported. Tomorrow they had to film in Prague-Nusle, where she had lived after arriving from Vienna, and then they would go to Terezín for four days. They really need Milena as a translator; all the contacts they'd brought from Israel had fallen through. They even tried to convince Kristýna to take this trip; according to their script, she was supposed to escort them around the places where she and Berta had become friends. But they had thought up the script without her, she told them. She would not go north, and never to Terezín. She wasn't going to loaf around hotels, and she had work to do at home. She'd already told them what she had, and they were not going to film her crying. This they were counting on: that the old woman would tear up and endow the film with the necessary pathos. They told her that the house where Berta had lived in the countryside was still standing, as well as the train station she'd painted from the window. She'd always lived in buildings near a train station. Even the window was still there, perhaps with the varnish she'd touched and which had preserved the molecules of her skin. The window to the south, the sill with the vase of flowers, and her bright bouquet of begonias on a warm, lazy, small-town afternoon when the world stopped turning and between lunch and dinner stretched an insurmountable expanse of silken, viscous time. In the year 1941.

Milena said she would go; at least she could make some money for the holidays. She could disappear from school for as long as she wanted. No one would notice anyway. Viki told Milena they would meet up tomorrow at nine in front of Berta's house in Nusle. Viki was the director's wife, production manager, and script girl all in one. Milena has to help them find Berta's apartment and try to get the people who still lived there to let them in.

Milena is twenty-five years old. Two years ago, she moved out of her parents' house and into her grandmother's. She doesn't have enough to rent her own place. She is studying French and English and hopes someday she'll make it as a translator. Quite an attractive girl. She says she's oversensitive and writes poems because they help her cope with life. By life, she means men.

She knows nothing about Berta Altmann except that she was a painter, a friend of her grandmother, and a Jew who sometime long ago died in a concentration camp with other Jews.

She's sitting in a tram heading for Nusle, a little nervous, and looking forward to new adventures. Yesterday something flashed between her and the cameraman, whose exotic name she still has not managed to recall. They'd noticed each other. They hesitated for a moment, and since then have been aware of each other's existence. It's so exciting, that first contact. You can't even call it a glance, thinks Milena, but, rather, a caress from a distance. She likes to think in the tram. Letting herself be carried along, her eyes slipping over the images outside without alighting on any one thing for long. Like a film reel—a film of the May streets of Prague.

It's not even nine o'clock, but the sun is already blazing

down. The beginning of May is hot; everything fades too quickly, thinks Milena. Everything smells so wonderful, so nice. Her stomach is clenching up, just like before an exam. It's that cameraman.

They're waiting for her in front of an old apartment building; there are only three of them. They didn't hire the soundman and the lighting technician today. Viki and her husband, Noah, are looking up and counting the floors. Viki has a reproduction of a picture that Berta painted from the window of this building. It shows tracks, the station building, and the roof of the house opposite. By the angle, they're trying to figure out which apartment she lived in. They're going to have to ring several doorbells before they locate it. Fortunately, it's Saturday and people will be home. And they'll be pleasantly pissed off, thinks Milena. The still-nameless cameraman is grumpy in the morning. He hardly even acknowledges her. Not a trace of yesterday's spark. He's digging around in one of his satchels and cursing beneath his breath. How can he work without an assistant? He can't change the filters and carry the camera and tripod all by himself. If you don't have money, you shouldn't make movies, he says under his breath, and by that he means Viki and her husband. But these two apparently know his morning moods and don't react to his insults. They just wait for it to pass.

The building has six floors and they start on the fourth at random. The cameraman takes a seat on the steps in front of the building—let them come and get him when they find it. He's not going to drag himself upstairs and loiter about in front of doors.

What an annoying guy, thinks Milena. And he looks older than he did yesterday—he's at least forty. She's standing in front of a stranger's door, with Viki and Noah behind her. She must not think about the awkwardness of her task. She just rings the doorbell and, as soon as it opens, quickly spits out what they're here for. She has to speak quickly enough that the woman or man inside doesn't have time to protest while Viki and Noah squeeze past her into the apartment and compare the view from the window with the reproduction.

Contrary to their assumptions, they finally locate the window on the third floor. A woman around fifty and her mother inhabit Berta's previous apartment. An antiseptic aroma of lonely women wafts from the upholstery, drapes, crocheted furniture covers, and tablecloths. When did they move in here? The old lady muses out loud: Right after the war. Her husband had been a clerk for the railway. The daughter is making coffee in a porcelain pot decorated with roses, and she apologizes that they don't have any cake; they had been about to make one today for Sunday. They're delighted, as if the film people's visit was intended for them, and they listen, captivated, to Berta's story. She probably painted that. The old lady points to a little sketch of Nusle houses that hangs in the corner above the television set. It was here when we moved in. Her husband had it framed. And when did the artist move out—in '38? Milena doesn't know the details, but she makes something up merely to entertain the women and keep them from noticing what's going on behind them.

The cameraman's annoyance has passed. With Noah's assistance, he shifts the armchairs and takes down the curtains. Then he opens the window all the way and orders Viki to slowly move one of the casements until the pane reflects the railway building, tracks, and building opposite. It takes an awfully long time, and Milena is starting to run out of energy and topics of conversation. When they finally start to pack up, she is utterly exhausted.

That's enough for today, Viki announces as they exit the

building. Now Milena will go to lunch with them and then they'll take her home, so she'll have time to pack for tomorrow's trip.

In the car, a van with room for six people, the cameraman asks her what she was talking so loudly about with those woman and if she really had to run off at the mouth the whole time. I like it quiet when I work, he says. He looks at her through narrowed eyes, gauging her anger.

Leave her alone, says Viki from the front seat.

The cameraman shrugs his shoulders, stretches out his legs, and closes his eyes. Prague interests him only through the lens of a video camera. His name is Aaron.

It's Milena's first trip to Terezín. Strangely enough, they hadn't gone there on a field trip or talked about this aspect of the war in school, unlike the Great Patriotic War and the liberation by the Red Army. Reticence concerning the Holocaust was probably connected with the animosity toward the state of Israel— the "reactionary state of Israel," Milena recalls, was the only way Israel was referred to in the textbooks. What did *reactionary* actually mean? She had no idea and it never occurred to her to look into it. During communism certain words simply arose in established combinations, like the *imperialist West* or the *Bloc of Peace*. No one took the textbooks seriously, just like the entire school, the government, and everything connected with it. It didn't make sense to bother your head over it.

After the revolution, history was discussed primarily with reference to the restitution of property confiscated after 1948, and by the time the Holocaust and other taboo subjects made their way into the history books, Milena had long since finished high school. In college, there wasn't any Czech history.

Until she was twenty-three, Milena had had no reason to

care about this place. She hadn't even known where Terezín was, and now she's surprised it's so close to Prague. In her mind, it was always somewhere on the Polish border.

It's a weekday and the town surrounded by parapets is calm and deserted. Each building looks like the next; false windows peer out at the streets. Trees on the main square, green gates, cobblestones on the thoroughfare, stairs. The former women's sleeping quarters have been converted into apartments.

They ring at a door, and a young woman holding a baby opens. She lets them in, and while Aaron films the view from the window, she talks about Terezín.

They lured us here with apartments and work, and now almost all of us are on relief, she says. You can't make anything off the tourists. You think people feel like wasting their money here? They take one look around and then vanish; they don't even want to spend the night here. Last year they closed the hotel. I'm not surprised. I know this is supposed to be a memorial, but what's that got to do with us? When soldiers were garrisoned here, things were still pretty lively—pubs and shops—but now everything's dead.

Viki gives the woman some money, and with Milena's help, asks if they might come back. In a week, they have a meeting in Prague with three women who lived in this very room as children, and she would like to bring them here.

You know, we don't really take an interest in what did or didn't happen here, says the woman. But feel free to come back. We're always home anyway.

Milena is dreaming. She's lying in a white fog, bordered by black hummocks of volcanic hills. Between the hills run train tracks. Between the hills run narrow paths. Aaron is leading her, leading her along a thin, fine thread; all around she senses living beings, condensed light, weeping. She knows where he's leading her. Suddenly, the thread snaps and everything vanishes; she's speechless, naked, alone, naked, in a crevasse.

She wakes up in a disproportionately tall hotel in relation to the dimensions of the town, on the twelfth floor. Yesterday she surreptitiously opened the door to a small deck, which was probably meant to be a balcony, but it had remained only an intimation of one, a little concrete slab without a railing, overlooking the entire Central Bohemian Uplands. She took a seat on the doorsill, stretched out her legs on the concrete, and smoked a cigarette. That's how he found her. He himself had given up smoking years ago, but now he felt like imitating this movement as well as the way she ran her thumb over her upper lip, her concentration on the glowing tip of the cigarette. The stark shadow of the mountain above the city was lengthening. Litoměřice was going out, roof by roof.

She wakes up just before six, fully refreshed, gets dressed, and takes the elevator down. She sets out into the empty streets, which remind her of a labyrinth open on all sides. She crosses the river, climbs the steps along the cracked and chipped church, turns left, and halts at the ramparts. She rests her hands on the low wall. The sun mounts the sky, sparkling through tears that suddenly fill her eyes. She is not crying from sadness, but from the burning sensation of life.

He's interested in his work, nothing else!

Today they're filming prisoners' drawings in the Terezín museum. Some were done by well-known artists who were imprisoned here with the most famous composers, musicians, writers, actors, scientists, and philosophers of their time. On the artistic and intellectual side, the Terezín prisoners could have been living in luxury.

Aaron is trying to concentrate on individual operations: the light, the composition of the shot, the brightness. He cannot allow his emotions to control him, and they don't. He's slept off the previous day's irritation. Yesterday he allowed himself to get carried away, which is something he cannot permit himself, not if he wants to do his work well and earn the rather large sum of money Viki and Noah are paying him. He's not cheap, because he's good. And he's good because he puts everything into his work.

Young girls, he muses, are always asking about feelings. Of course I have feelings; otherwise, I wouldn't know what or how to film. But it's all about keeping them under control. But young girls don't want to understand this, and they do everything to make you lose control.

She asked him what kind of feelings he has in Terezín.

Hatred, he said.

Hatred for whom? she asked.

The Germans and everyone who allowed this to happen.

She asked where he was from, as if that mattered. No, his family hadn't been in a concentration camp. He's a Sephardic Jew; his parents had gone to Israel from Morocco because they didn't want to live among Arabs anymore. That's why he especially doesn't understand how any Jews could have returned to Germany after the war and still insist that they do not harbor any hatred for the country. How can they live there? And sleep in peace?

But that was a long time ago, she said, and this upset him. What has it been, fifty or sixty years? The older he gets, the shorter seem those fifty or sixty years. Milena doesn't understand that this hatred is like a memory, and one has a duty to hate. If he stops hating the murderers, it would be like forgiving them. Which is the same thing as forgetting. If he ceases to hate, the sacrifice of millions of human lives would cease to exist.

She smoked in silence. And then patted him on the shoulder. This he perceived as another attack, but perhaps she meant well.

He looks around and doesn't see Milena in the hall.

He goes back to the drawings of his tortured and murdered people. Pencil or charcoal on bits of packing paper—there had obviously been a shortage of paper in Terezín, as well. A line for food, trees on a square that look charred, a still life with brooms and pails, a garret with hanging laundry. He finds the drawings from the sleeping quarters the most intriguing. In a long room, bunk beds are aligned right next to one another, and each bed is like a tiny island or miniature boat: All of their occupants had to stuff everything they needed to survive into a small space, and so the beds were strewn and hung with the greatest variety of objects: cups, clothing, rope, bags, and even pictures. Aaron focuses his camera and at the same time wonders if, in the end, such a bed wouldn't be enough for him, too. He's always on the road anyway.

Then she asked him if he thought he would have survived a concentration camp.

Survival is a question of will and the organization of life's essentials, he replied.

So you would have?

If I was lucky on top of everything else, he responded.

I wouldn't, said Milena, and laughed.

He didn't understand her laughter nor the ease with which she had given up on the need to survive. He told himself that these people, people like her, never had to struggle for anything, and that's why they lacked the perseverance and strength to fight. But then he remembered that not long ago communism had ruled this country, and he tried to imagine what it had been like and if it required any special fortitude. He was afraid to ask, since he might look like an idiot. She was too young to know anything about it anyway.

Milena is walking through the museum. Among the heaps of documents is the typewritten proposal for the Final Solution of the Jewish question from the second half of the 1930s, including typos. And letters as well, stating that the International Red Cross is concerned about whether the Terezín concentration camp has good hygienic conditions. From this, she understands that the Jews who were left in Europe survived by mistake, a mistake in planning and a lack of time. And also that the extermination proceeded under international supervision. She examines the lists of prisoners and people scheduled for transport and sees that alongside Czech names are Slovak, German, Dutch, Danish, and French ones. The documentation is certainly in good order; nothing is missing. The paper hasn't even begun to yellow.

She stares at the corrected typos the longest.

They finish at the museum around four, but the day's not over. Aaron has decided he has to climb up the church bell tower and film Terezín from a bird's-eye view. The tower is locked, so Milena has to look for the key. Fortunately, she finds it even before the sun begins to set.

They climb the wooden stairs; Milena helps Aaron with his satchels. Noah stayed behind because he suffers from vertigo, and Viki excused herself and said she would use the time to take care of some important phone calls.

They don't stop until they reach the very top. The bell tower is open on all four sides so that the sound of the bell can resound in all directions. It's not meant for the public and there's no railing. The bell is heavy and still. This is the first time Milena has seen such a large bell up close. Aaron adjusts the camera and tries to get the best shots; he tries not to think about the abyss yawning beneath him. The only way to avoid getting dizzy is to concentrate on what he's doing. The sun is already quite low, the light substantial, ideal. He takes in the town square, the file of houses, the barracks, the street corners, the distant ramparts with green grass, and the fields beyond. From here, you can also see the nearest train stop, from which the Terezín prisoners had to continue on foot. The threads of the railroad tracks shimmer like copper.

Suddenly, the tower shudders; Aaron staggers and almost falls out. Of course he holds on to the camera firmly. It's only for a moment, and he quickly calms himself and turns around. The clapper slams into the iron side of the bell with a deafening din. Milena is standing beneath the bell and holding on to a rope, paralyzed. She's gone completely white.

Aaron turns off the camera and slowly begins packing his things. His hands are shaking so much that he wouldn't be able to film anything anyway. The racket slowly dies away. There's no point in yelling at her. She could have killed him. He finishes packing and wordlessly begins to descend the stairs. He doesn't look around and assumes that the stupid girl is behind him. But she's not. He calls out. Not a sound comes from above. Cursing, he turns around with his camera and equipment and climbs back up. He finds her collapsed by a wooden column, curled up into a ball, her hands covering her face, shaking and weeping.

At first, he thinks she's crying for him, for how she frightened him. He puts aside his things, sits down next to her, and carefully touches her shoulder.

It wasn't so bad, he says. You didn't do it on purpose. I'm not angry with you.

It's horrible, sobs Milena. I can't understand how something like this could have happened!

This sounds naive to him, but he feels ashamed. He doesn't want to be condescending. She's right, he says to himself, but you can't allow yourself to get like this. I grew up with the idea of the Holocaust and have gotten used to it.

Crying's too easy, he tells Milena. We could bawl from morning to night, but that doesn't lead anywhere. On the contrary, one must draw strength from this horror.

Milena slowly calms down, asks Aaron for a tissue, and blows her nose. Then they go back down.

It's almost dark when they get back to Litoměřice. They'll eat something in the first restaurant they happen upon on the way to the hotel. They're so tired, they don't care what they eat. They part at the reception desk; Milena goes up to the twelfth floor and immediately heads for her cement perch. She's almost certain he'll come over. But it will take him a while; he has to pretend he couldn't fall asleep. The night is warm; the aroma from the fruit orchards rises and hangs in the air above the city.

She hears footsteps behind her. They halt at the door to the balcony and go no farther. Maybe it's not him. Milena gets frightened and turns around. Aaron smiles apologetically. Am I bothering you? I couldn't sleep.

I couldn't sleep, either, Milena says, lying.

He sits down in the doorway so he doesn't have to look across the edge of the platform.

I get vertigo, he says. When I'm not looking through my camera lens.

She's half-turned away from him; he sees her profile. Her long blond hair is disheveled and held together by a clasp. He looks at her neck and then lightly places an open palm on it.

It is just as he'd feared. The girl is soft and warm; the touch provides him with disproportionate delight. He removes his hand.

I'm divorced, he says, and I have an eight-year-old son from my marriage. I love him intensely.

Of course, says Milena.

I have a girlfriend, continues Aaron. It's my first serious girl-friend since my divorce. She's thirty-four, a photographer.

Irrelevant, thinks Milena, and says it aloud: Irrelevant.

What? Aha, replies Aaron. He presumed it would be fair and gentlemanlike to tell her how things stood. Just so she knows. On the other hand, by saying this he implied—what did he imply? That he wants to sleep with her, but in such a way that there'll be no claims. That's what he meant. He feigns a yawn and stands up. Milena gets up, too.

He accompanies her to the door and kisses her cheek. Like an uncle, he thinks.

Like an uncle, he says out loud, and hopes she will contra-dict him. But Milena disappears wordlessly into her room and leaves him with the excruciating feeling that he's old and stupid, and his attempt to become close utterly failed.

The next day, they continue heading northeast. In Hronov they locate Berta's apartment, actually two apartments. One two-room flat overlooking the train station, where a young Roma family now lives. The other is an attic garret, to which Berta and her husband had to move for the final six months before the transport. Nobody has lived in it since then, and amid the junk that has accumulated here for more than fifty years you can recognize the ruins of a room: a shred of green print curtain, the frame of an armchair gnawed away by mice, what they used to call a wing chair, a fragment of a lamp with a blue paper lamp shade.

They sleep in a hotel called Na Vyhlídce, halfway between Náchod and Hronov.

The following day, they visit a farmhouse in the hills above Hronov, where Berta used to go to paint landscapes. An old housewife remembers her and her husband. She shows them a photo album, makes them coffee, and assails them with a great many cakes. A few paces from the farmhouse is the boundary line where Berta used to draw the panorama composed of a row of fruit trees, a shallow valley, and the distant outline of the mountains. Somebody had photographed her on this spot. Hands in her pockets and wearing a light-colored overcoat and a knit beret, she is surveying the scene like a general on the eve of battle. A fox terrier lies at her feet, obviously waiting for Berta to bend down and scratch her.

Once again, they go to Terezín. This time, they had to rent a small bus; besides Viki, Noah, Aaron, and Milena, a Czech soundman and three old women who survived the Holocaust and who remember Berta are going with them.

One lives in Bohemia, one flew over from the United States, and the third came from Israel. They didn't travel this far for Noah's film, but because a meeting of those who had been children in Terezín happens to be taking place in Prague.

Noah found out about the gathering when he was in Tel Aviv and incorporated it into the screenplay.

Terezín children in the ballroom of the Prague Railway Union House, wrinkled faces behind tables adorned with ironed tablecloths. Friends sit next to one another, and muffled giggling can be heard throughout the ballroom. Perhaps they're nudging one another beneath the tables. The eldest person present used to be their schoolteacher; he remembers them both by their names and their nicknames and even today addresses them from a position of authority: Now, each one of you will stand up, introduce yourself, give your year of deportation, how old you were, then state your barracks number and the name of your closest friends. Then tell us briefly about where you live, what you do, how many children and grandchildren you have, and so on. Why don't you start, Suzi.

A diminutive woman with gaudily painted lips and meticulously permed hair takes the floor and begins speaking with a slight accent: I'm Zuzana Růžičková, Suzi. I lived in female barracks L four ten, room number twenty-six. My best friends were Lucinka Hořejší and Marianka Lustigová; our beds were next to one another. They both died in Auschwitz. Lucinka and I were thirteen, Marianka a year older. I arrived in Terezín with my parents in February 1942. Just before the transport to the east, I got sick and had to be quarantined. My parents and brother, however, left. I never saw them again. After the war, I studied in Prague and then, after 1948, in Paris. There I met my husband, also a Czech, and we moved together to Israel. We live in Jerusalem. Until just recently I worked as a pediatrician, and now I'm retired. I have two children, a son and a daughter. My son is also a doctor, and my daughter is a painter. I have two grandchildren.

The three women in the bus are chatting together, recalling individual faces and words. They're finding enjoyment in the images unearthed from their mutual memory, as if they belonged to an ordinary childhood and not one spent in Terezín. Aaron films them from the aisle.

Then he sits down next to Milena and says, Can you tell me what these women are talking about? I understand only that it's about Terezín. And I can see that they're laughing, as if they'd been at summer camp instead of a concentration camp.

They're remembering people they used to know, what

someone looked like, what they said, who liked whom. They're recalling certain wisecracks, says Milena. Is the intensity of happy moments reinforced by the unhappiness that accompanies them? Were you ever genuinely happy? she asks.

Yes, when my son was born, but then I didn't pay any attention to it, he says. And you?

I don't know, she replies. I can't remember any great happiness or unhappiness; everything was always somehow incomplete.

The bus halts at the square, not far from a building with green gates.

The three women go first, and behind them Aaron with his camera and the soundman with his microphone on a long pole, then Noah, and finally Viki and Milena. They climb the steps to the foyer, which leads to the living quarters. Here is where we would leave our shoes, says one of the women, and here, do you remember? Here stood pails of water. They knock on the door. This time, the husband is home; the young woman and child have gone off somewhere. Apparently, he wants to collect money from the film people himself.

The three women remove their shoes at the threshold and reverently go inside. They look around. The room has been preserved. Here's where our beds were, the table where we drew with Berta. She would come see us for our painting lessons. It was like a holiday for us, and we really looked forward to them. We could forget about everything at least for a moment. She would bring us pieces of various materials, small pieces of wood and newspaper for collages, paper and paint. I don't know where she managed to find it all. She let the younger children simply play among themselves, but she would assign us older girls different tasks. She taught us about colors, shapes, and perspective. But she never criticized; she was all praise.

I never would have thought I had any talent, one of them

says, laughing. In school, they always said I had two left hands. But she insisted that I had a special way of seeing the world and that I could become an artist.

Do you remember what she looked like? asks Noah. What kind of effect did she have on you?

The women all contribute to the image: She was small, says one, shorter than some of us. She had thick, short hair and luminous dark brown eyes. She was always bright and cheerful, says another, full of energy. She was always coming up with more and more ideas. She probably had quite a good time with us, too. She was especially kind, says a third. We all loved her.

After they leave the room, they want to explore the building. On the steps, they find the spot where they had carved their initials, and downstairs, in the hallway to the basement, they point out the place where Berta arranged an exhibition for them. She brought pieces of old sacks, fastened them to the wall, and hung up the pictures.

They join hands and spin around, singing the anthem of their sleeping quarters. In our room was a wonderful bunch, she says. We sewed ourselves a flag, and when the first ones from our group started leaving for the east, we cut it up into pieces, and each of us took one with us. We swore we would someday meet again and put it back together. The women pull out three small pieces of material, place them next to one another, and step back so Aaron can film it. Something is written on the flag, but you cannot make out the words—too much is missing.

On the way back to Prague toward evening, Aaron takes a seat next to Milena, apparently as a matter of course. As if the sacrifice of not sleeping with her gives him a right to everything else. They are driving past bright yellow rapeseed fields. The cameraman has turned off his camera and for a long time just stares out the window, observing the countryside. How adorable, he thinks in English, and is surprised he knows such a word. Soft and suffused with moisture. He feels like stopping. Leaving everything, getting out of the bus, and stretching out beneath one of the lush green trees.

Aaron has the last day off. Viki and Noah have decided to relax in the hotel. In the afternoon, they will go out for a little walk, but they don't want to get tied up anywhere for long. They're tired. One day of peace before they head back to Tel Aviv, and that merry-go-round awaiting them will do them good.

Aaron wants Milena to show him the Prague Jewish Town. Although they already filmed there in the museum, he wants to see it again, just for himself. They walk down the street past the cemetery and just peer over the fence. Aaron doesn't want to pay the expensive entrance fee. Milena tells him that before the revolution there was no entrance fee. When she was a little girl, they used to go for walks on Sunday to the Jewish cemetery. They would collect stones on the way from Dejvice, which they would then use to decorate the nameless graves, as well as that of Rabbi Loew, who even dead performed miracles. That's why he always had the most stones. Some gravestones were completely sunk into the ground, with only the top protruding; others were tumbled over, dislodged by the abundance of newer slabs jostling for their place. Unlike Christian cemeteries, it was all a mysterious tangle, and she found it fascinating, most of all the fact that the dead were buried layer upon layer, and the entire cemetery was an accumulation rising ever upward, the earth, displaced by decomposing bodies, piled up in massive embankments overgrown with ivy and drifts of fallen leaves.

Before the revolution, Milena recalls, the Jewish cemetery was the most deserted place in the old part of Prague. I was always afraid they would lock us in by accident.

As they cross Mánes Bridge, with a view encompassing the white spires of Strahov Monastery and Petřín Hill, Aaron ventures to ask why in Litoměřice she was so convinced that she wouldn't survive a concentration camp.

She replies after a long pause, which Aaron fills by wondering if the bridge's architect had intended the semicircular stone landing they were standing on as a kissing spot.

Because I'm not real enough.

You mean brave?

No, real. It's just that I often think I don't exist in the proper way. Like I'm some sort of . . . reflection. She points to the surface of the water. It's hard to explain. My grandmother, for example, doesn't get it at all. She says I'm still searching. But that's not true. I'll never be like her. She never has any doubts as to who she is or what she does. She thinks she's actually searching for something through her art, that she's moving toward some sort of truth that is important for her and everyone else. She claims she doesn't believe in anything, but she believes a lot; otherwise, she couldn't have endured what she did. She wouldn't have let the Communists punish her; she wouldn't have had to go work in a factory. I think she'd give her life for her art. Could you give your life for anything?

For Israel, he replies without hesitation. And for my son.

And I . . . probably couldn't for anything, says Milena. Nothing that would be so important to me.

And that's why you wouldn't survive?

That's what I'm trying to say. Do you see that boat? It stirs up the surface and what happens? The reflection is fragmented. I would come apart at the first actual confrontation. I know I would. The ones who survived are completely different. They're like my grandmother.

You're still really young. At your age, you don't cling to

life, because you can't imagine death. Unless you deal with it every day.

And I have bad eyesight.

How bad? asks Aaron.

Really bad. Without my contacts, all I see are blurry smudges.

This apparently gratifies Aaron. The physical defect brings the girl closer to him. She's helpless and thus needs his protection.

I read that in Terezín people with glasses went straight to the gas chambers. Someone who managed to take off his glasses in time had to pretend he could see. Can you imagine? You grope your way about and one false step could spell death. Marina Tsvetaeva didn't wear glasses, either, but out of pride.

Who?

You know, the poet, says Milena.

Aaron senses more and more that Milena is disappointed and bored. In the morning, they were chatting, observing the passersby, and always laughing at something. Even during lunch, they were in good spirits. But now the afternoon is passing more quickly than he expected. Words are a waste of time; he doesn't want to go anywhere, do anything, tackle another topic. He wants to sit here with her in this quiet café, where they won't be disturbed, and just look, record every detail, every irregularity of her face, her freckles. He must be certain that the image he takes away with him is utterly faithful.

He will have to look for a long time. Rehearse in his mind what he saw and then verify it according to reality. Adjust what his memory got wrong, right now when she's sitting directly across from him. Aaron does not trust his memory. Even this makes him nervous. He knows he shouldn't remain silent. Young women immediately think you're stupid and have nothing to say. He longs to caress her while he can. We should make love, Aaron thinks to himself over and over. In the hours they have left. He would never forgive himself the lost opportunity as long as he lived. They should go back to the hotel right now and make love. Why doesn't he say it? And why doesn't she suggest it herself? Can't she sense how agonizing the situation is?

Instead, Milena broaches a new subject; she asks him something and he has to answer. The most interesting film he's ever made. Then she asks what his plans are for next year. Does he have any brothers and sisters? Describe the desert to her. Is this girl crazy? Does she think she can learn anything about him this way? Their conversation is coming apart; crevasses emerge, wider and deeper, as every word snaps off another piece of time.

Do you want to come back with me to the hotel?

She didn't understand, or maybe she didn't hear him.

Do you want to come back with me to the hotel? he asks in English. It sounds repulsive. Why do they have to make themselves understood in this horrible English!

The girl nods her affirmation and he waves to the waiter for the check.

It was the first time he'd permitted himself to use this word in his thoughts, and the very next moment he has to ask her: Is this love?

Milena lies silently at his side. She's run out of words; he, on the other hand, feels like telling her everything. He would read her his childhood diaries if he had any. He would tell her about his first love. Instead, he is talking about Israel, his son, whom he's afraid for. He'd most like to take him away somewhere to safety, where every other moment a busload of children doesn't fly off into the air. Children are endangered the most. He would take him away, but he's not allowed to; he's not allowed to leave the borders of the country with him. This was decided by the court, which granted custody to his former wife.

He talks about his fear of unforeseeable death. A few years ago, he was filming with a director in Sarajevo, or, rather, in the wreckage that was left of Sarajevo. Just after the end of the siege. The director was looking for similarities between life in the bombarded city and life in Israel. He wanted to find out how people behaved, those who were well aware that they could die at any moment.

Apparently, at the beginning of the siege, they were thinking all the time: Should I go quickly or slowly? Will they shoot me if I cross the street here or at the corner? They tried to put themselves in the mind of the enemy. They were driven insane by the thought that a few steps before or a few steps after awaited a death, a death they could have avoided. After a few months, however, they calmed down and realized that, as far as death was concerned, it was all the same. They entrusted themselves to the will of a higher power, which ruled the actions of the men concealed in the hills around Sarajevo.

Almost everyone they interviewed in Sarajevo agreed that living in a besieged city was ghastly and beautiful at the same time. This was not a contradiction. Love prospered most of all because people wanted to catch up with what they'd missed and experience something beautiful right now. And the theater. The theater was packed every night. They longed to forget everything just for a moment and enjoy one another's company, to hear their own voices, their laughter, to touch one another, be close to one another, and experience the fullness of life. That was what he heard most often: to experience the fullness of life.

After three years, some of them had succeeded in digging a tunnel out of Sarajevo, Aaron is telling her. It came out just beyond the blockade. So the Serbs wouldn't notice anything, they had to escape at night, one at a time and with a minimal amount of baggage. The tunnel was low, and part of the way they had to crawl on all fours. I met people who had actually made it. They managed to escape that hell, then went to France or Holland and even got asylum. But they were unhappy. They couldn't stand it. After a few months, they crawled on all fours back through the tunnel.

I couldn't stay away from Israel long, either, says Aaron, not until it calms down. But will it ever calm down? We were born under siege; we grew up in it. What if the idea of change actually frightens us?

Of course, the people of Sarajevo were also glad when the siege ended five years later. But they also admitted they had gotten used to the strain, and now ordinary life seemed unexpectedly barren. All of a sudden, they had too much time for everything and didn't know what to do with it. Renew the rituals of social intercourse? Marriage and routine, which quickly palls? The idea of ordinary life and everyday worries depressed them. Illnesses and traffic accidents seemed ridiculous. It was as if the possibility of instant death was an addictive drug. Like playing Russian roulette, says Aaron.

They don't settle on or agree to anything. They don't promise each other they'll ever meet again. They fall asleep, and when they awake, Milena has to leave quickly because she doesn't want to run into Viki and Noah. They barely have time to exchange addresses.

As they say good-bye, Aaron pulls her toward him and says, I belong to you.

Milena has always imagined that the word *belong* represents something improper. She has never wanted to belong to anybody and has resolved to reject anyone who wants to belong to her. To her, belonging to someone implies ownership. But she has nothing against what is going on here. Let Aaron go ahead and belong to her, in Israel. She has had a good time with him. She's not sorry. She has to go.

Milena softly closes the door behind her and walks down the long hotel corridor. She has a pleasant feeling of lightness and is glad she does not have to deal with what was supposed to happen next; she won't have to wait for Aaron's phone call or, conversely, wonder if and when she should call him. She doesn't have to agonize over him. His departure will resolve everything elegantly.

She decides to walk home. It's a marvelous and bright, sunny morning. She has a cup of coffee in the Old Town and then buys a dress in a boutique with the money that Viki paid her the day before yesterday. She originally wanted a red dress, but then she took a fancy to a blue-green one, something between the sky and the summer sea. Whenever she puts it on, she'll remember Aaron.

At eleven o'clock, precisely when the airplane with Aaron, Noah, and Viki is lifting off from Ruzyně Airport, Milena is beset with fatigue. And, concomitantly, a feeling of cruel and sudden loss. How far away is Israel anyway? Awfully far. Apart from everything else.

CHAPTER 2

Friends

A GIRL IN VIENNA, 1914. She's just turned fourteen. She grew up without a mother and feels more mature than her peers. And more alone. Disjointedly, but all the more intensively, she perceives everything going on around her. She doesn't think about it. She drinks in everything, like a mushroom, without discrimination, without a teacher; she hungers after everything that resonates with her inner pulsation, with her longing, with her trepidation.

War will be declared in a few days, but the girl is much more interested in other things. Is she really as ugly as the mirror seems to suggest? Will she ever finally fall in love? And could anyone ever fall in love with her? For now, she perceives these two matters separately.

And furthermore, does she have any talent? Will she become a great artist?

Her father steers her creativity and undeniable talents in a practical direction. She should study photography. He's not rich and would welcome the certainty that she'll soon be able to support herself. Also, he has two small children with his second wife.

Berta quite enjoys photography, but she feels it's only the beginning. She doesn't want to confine the world to black and white and the gamut of grays in between. She longs for colors, experiences them almost physically. She can fall in love with a color and then she wants to surround herself entirely with it. She sews dresses and thinks up food in the color. If she loves green, she's ready to cast aside all others and worship only green in all its shades and tones until her interest is exhausted and she develops a passion for another. It's like that with everything she sets her mind to. So at sixteen years of age, she decides to give up photography and applies to the Academy of Applied Arts. For a while, she considered the Academy of Fine Arts, but she knew her father would never contribute to something as abstract as painting. Besides, the Academy of Fine Arts has the reputation of an ossified and pedantic institution that expels every real artist, or else they run away themselves, like Egon Schiele. Genuine struggles take place elsewhere, and modern teachers give priority to art trades. Berta signs up for one of them, the textile workshop, where, besides drafting and working with colors, she learns to weave, design patterns, and handle different materials. It's actually quite suitable; she enjoys holding something solid in her hands. And now in Vienna, a lot of painters are seriously designing wall coverings, dishes, and furniture. It is related to the new art, the attempt to remold human life and its industrially produced elements into an artistic work. To preserve the spirit in places from which it rapidly flees. Or something like that.

In 1916, there's nothing to eat, and most men in Berta's neighborhood have had to enlist. She and her classmate Maja swear eternal loyalty to each other and cut their hair in celebration of the funeral of Franz Joseph and the Austro-Hungarian monarchy.

A year later, Maja's brother Rudi takes his sister and her friend to the Café Central. They enter with trepidation and thumping hearts, as if into a temple of some unknown, fantastic god. The ranks of devotees are somewhat spare due to the war, but nevertheless they see with their own eyes several men whose names are enswathed in an arousing aura of both the damned and the elect.

The girls do not really understand all these new artistic ideas and trends, but they rave about them all the more passionately and disdain their hometown for its philistinism, sentimentality, and poorly concealed bourgeois character. They hate waltzes, the smell of potatoes in the passageways, Hanswurst, the monarchy, beer houses, and military music. They hate the ostentatious tone of Viennese critics who are prepared to tear down everything they don't understand. As soon as they finish their studies, they will flee to Berlin. Even Prague is more unfettered, they say.

The painter K., about whom Berta is most curious, is not in the café. He joined the emperor's cavalry voluntarily, fought on the eastern front, and was shot in the head. He's been lying in some Polish hospital for a year. His lover sits here instead, at whose insistence, as all of Vienna is aware, the painter K. enlisted.

Rudi assigns names to the unfamiliar faces: the writers Zweig and Broch, Altenberg and von Hofmannsthal. Some of them have stayed in Vienna because they are serving out their duties in the military press office. They publish newspapers teeming with patriotic babble and stories of heroism by Austrian soldiers. They stoke the fires of insanity with their own brains. I'd rather let myself be shot for treason, says Rudi exasperated, who is too young for conscription.

The young man with distinctive eyes and a delicate, feminine countenance sitting next to the former lover of the painter K. is the poet Mendel from Prague. Recently arrived in Vienna and also in the press office, he is starting to make a name for himself. They say he's her new favorite, but nothing is known for certain. She's quite recently divorced. Her husband, the architect Czerny, was her lover even when husband number one, a famous composer, was still alive. When she became a widow, she had a brief affair with the painter K., but his intensity and infatuation obviously grew tiresome. Why else would she have gone back to the tedious architect and even married him? Now he's also at the front, narrates Rudi in a whisper. Neatly tidied away.

The Viennese femme fatale seems impossibly old to Berta and Maja. A corpulent madam who surely still wears a corset. A sugar loaf.

The painter K.'s mother, whispers Rudi, when she could no longer stand looking at her son's obsession, used to lay in wait in front of her house with a revolver.

What's so special about that woman? The girls try to deduce it from the admiring looks of the poet, who is supposedly to become her next victim.

Hear ye, hear ye, says Maja, is it perhaps due to the influence of Dr. Freud that the entire male population of Vienna is obsessed with the urge to sleep with their own mothers?

Rudi is Maja's twin and they are a year younger than Berta—tall and slender, as if made of translucent wax. To Berta, who is dark, small, and robust, Maja seems marvelous, the genuine ideal of female beauty. She could look at her from morning till night, and even if they didn't say anything to each other and just sat there, she wouldn't consider the time spent with her in vain. Just the sight of her—light, changeable, blushing with an excitement that increases with the slightest trifle—always thrills her. Her brother, too—Maja's brother.

Maja has the ability to see things in their entirety. Such are her notions concerning dresses, hats, and cloaks, simple and integrated. Perfect silhouettes emerge in Maja's head, which Berta then provides with mass: material, colors, and patterns. Maja wants to become a famous fashion designer, and Berta will assist her if she can't make it as a painter.

She often goes to their house for dinner. Even during the war, the family of a high government official has a constant supply of food. The father is not around. He has not enlisted, but matters of state keep him occupied elsewhere. Nobody seems to mind. Maja and Rudi's mother even praises the war for denying her the pleasure of her husband's presence. Her name is Irena and she is originally from Croatia. She is tall and slender like her children. Unlike them, however, her eyes are black instead of blue, and her pupils are indistinguishable from her irises. Eyes like a squirrel, says Rudi. Mrs. Meyer is often preoccupied, but when she realizes that her children are around, she rouses herself from her daydreams and showers them with attention. She asks them about school and their plans and opinions, not in the judgmental or deprecatory tone that Berta's father speaks with her, but with genuine inquisitiveness. And on the piano she plays music by Beethoven and Debussy, Chopin and Mahler. Irena Meyer is still an excellent pianist, even though she had to renounce performing in public for the sake of her husband and his family.

Rudi is studying violin at the conservatory, but he wants to become a composer. He says that immediately after the war he's leaving for Berlin to become a student of Arnold Schönberg.

Maja and Rudi's mother suffers from depression and therefore avails herself of opium. Her children talk about it matter-of-factly and indulgently, as if she were the child. We just have to watch her so she doesn't overdo it, says Maja. She has her dreams. Who has the right to take them from her? They guard over her as if she were a rare crystal glass.

Berta loves their house, closed off from the cruelty and ugliness of war, the house where they speak passionately and seriously about only beautiful things, whether they be a hallucination, a clothing idea, or a musical phrase.

In the summer of 1918, Mrs. Meyer and her children move to a rented villa in Semmering. Irena longs to go to Dalmatia but can't get there because of the Italian front. At least the mountains, then. Even that can be dangerous, says Mr. Meyer, but Irena is suffocating in the city. Rudi coughs all winter, and Maja, too, is paler than usual. We don't want them to get tuberculosis, do we?

Even in Semmering, it's clear there's a war on, but much less so than in Vienna. In the mountain air, even the drab and mundane menu, for which the cook apologizes to Mrs. Meyer daily, seems more acceptable. If it were not for the closed-down hotels and empty and boarded-up villas, it would never occur to someone that nearby thousands of young men have been rotting alive in ditches for more than three years now.

Mrs. Meyer, who loves society, allows her children to invite whomever they want, and so nine young people meet at the villa—classmates from the Academy of Applied Arts and the conservatory. In mid-July, Professor Kurz arrives, a well-known figure in Viennese coffeehouses. He is an old friend of Mrs. Meyer, a philosopher. He has published two books, the second of which was a total flop with readers. It was a collection of one-line essays that turned everything upside down. He took great pride in their concision. "It seems that with this book the author sought to accomplish one thing: that the top can also be seen as the bottom. In this, he certainly succeeded. If we disregard the fact that he was standing on his head while writing this," wrote the literary critic Mucke.

Professor Kurz pretended that the rejection of his life's work affected him not in the least, but his friends claim that since then you can't talk to him. If he was eccentric before, now he is a downright curmudgeon. He argues all the time, and anyone he meets is an idiot. Now, when the monarchy has definitely sounded its last and intellectuals are projecting Communist revolution or democracy according to the American model, he is advocating aristocracy and vociferously declaring that if one is no better than the other, it would lead to the barbarization of everyone. Besides democracy, which according to him is the dictatorship of the blunder-headed, he also curses technological progress because it renders human life alien and soulless. On the other hand, he says, if someone asked me to choose between the automobile and Rilke's poems, I would invariably choose the automobile.

He likes only the young and can forgive them a lot. People are at their most ingenious at seventeen and eighteen, he says; then something happens to their brains. He also likes Mrs. Meyer. Apparently, there was something between them at one time, but not anymore. Only a faithful friendship has remained. Which doesn't mean that Mrs. Meyer doesn't sometimes feel like sending the disagreeable old geezer, as she refers to him in her mind, on the first train back to Vienna.

They've decided to put together a small orchestra and rehearse an opera over the summer. Something with a small cast, and if there are not enough voices, the singers can perform several parts at once. The artists will throw themselves into the stage sets and costume designs, and they will invite everyone who spends the summer in Semmering—friends and strangers alike. And why not? Let them come all the way from Vienna—they'll set up tents in the garden. This is the sole topic of conversation during mealtimes at the large table they've brought out onto the terrace. They just need to find an appropriate piece. Mrs. Meyer finally hits upon an idea. Years ago she saw Debussy's *Pelléas et Mélisande* in Paris. It was a chamber opera. but very creative nevertheless. Impressionism, says Rudi contemptuously, grimacing. His mother is offended: You won't find a more modern opera in all of Europe. Debussy broke every established compositional practice and far outstripped his time. At the Paris premiere sixteen years ago, it failed miserably with the bourgeois audience. It sounds compelling. That very afternoon, she orders the score from Vienna, along with Maeterlinck's play, which Debussy used as the libretto.

When the book arrives, everyone gathers on the terrace, and Mrs. Meyer reads aloud. She immediately translates the French original into German. Some already know the play, but it is as if they are hearing it for the first time now. Is it due to the warm evening, the fragrant evergreens and freshly mowed mountain meadows, or the excitement that possesses youth merely because they're together? The words strike them as magical, beautiful, profound. Yes, they tell themselves. That's how it should be. This is love. And there is no way to defend against it.

When Mrs. Meyer finishes reading, all is quiet. Dusk clambers from the valley up the dark, iridescent mountainside, while the peaks still reflect the final rays of the sun. It's almost as if footsteps can be heard among the shadowy larches at the far end of the garden. And they can see the dark silhouette flash by, bearing his sword.

> MÉLISANDE: *Ah! Il est derrière un arbre!*
> PELLÉAS: *Qui?*
> MÉLISANDE: *Goulaud!*
> PELLÉAS: *Goulaud? Ou donc? Je ne vois rien.*
> MÉLISANDE: *La . . . au bout de nos ombres.*

PELLÉAS: *Oui, oui; je l'ai vu . . . Ne nous retournons pas brusquement.*

MÉLISANDE: *Il a son épée.*

PELLÉAS: *Je n'ai pas la mienne.*

MÉLISANDE: *Il a vu que nous nous embrassions.*

PELLÉAS: *Il ne sait pas que nous l'avons vu. Ne bouge pas; ne tourne pas la tête. Il se précipiterait. Il nous observe. Il est encore immobile. Va-t'en, va-t'en, tout de suite par ici. Je l'attendrai, je l'arrêterai.*

MÉLISANDE: *Non!*

PELLÉAS: *Va-t'en!*

MÉLISANDE: *Non!*

PELLÉAS: *Il a tout vu. Il nous touera!*

MÉLISANDE: *Tant mieux!*

PELLÉAS: *Il vient!*

MÉLISANDE: *Tant mieux!*

PELLÉAS: *Ta bouche! Ta bouche!*

MÉLISANDE: *Oui! Oui! Oui!*

PELLÉAS: *Oh! Oh! Toutes les étoiles tombent!*

MÉLISANDE: *Sur moi aussi! Sur moi aussi!*

PELLÉAS: *Encore! Encore! Donne . . .*

MÉLISANDE: *Toute! . . . toute, toute!*

PELLÉAS: *. . . Donne, donne . . .*

(Goulaud se précipite et frappe Pelléas de son épée.)

MÉLISANDE: *Oh! Oh! Je n'ai pas de courage! Je n'ai pas de courage! Ah!*[1][*]

How are they to understand the cry: "I have not the courage! I have not the courage!"? Rudi, who has been charged with directing the entire production, racks his brains. Is it a belated reply to

---

[*] The translation for this text and subsequent passages in a foreign language appear on pages 219–221.

Pelléas's: "Give me, give me . . ."? Does it mean that Mélisande does not have the courage to give herself up entirely to her beloved? Or that she doesn't have the courage to die with him? Can it be both at the same time: I don't have the courage to give myself to you and I don't have the courage to die? Or: I don't have the courage to give you everything because I don't have the courage to die? Yes, decides Rudi, the final variant is the correct one. To give everything in love and to die are the same.

Maja and Elsa have taken charge of the costumes, Berta the masks, and, together with Ludwig, she designs the stage sets. In reality, however, everyone does everything, because they have to produce a unique and sensational work of art. The scenery cannot be realistic, no large castle hall, forest, grottoes, or cliffs. They work with cardboard and canvas, which must be colored and painted.

Dynamic abstraction, says Ludwig, who professes Kandinsky. The colors themselves will excite the imagination just as much as the music; they will evoke emotions and the images associated with them. It's like a science. Whereas in the first act Mélisande must be light blue, in the fourth I see her in dark red, and at the end, when she's dying, I see her as yellow. A conventional approach would clothe her in white to signify forgiveness and peace. But she is aching and dissolving in the light, the yellow blaze of the sun.

Or: At the beginning she'll be dark green, so she's barely visible in the forest. That's how Goulaud, who has lost his way, will find her. First he glimpses only an inconspicuous figure collapsed by a spring. Only when Mélisande lifts her head does he notice her and take fright: "How beautiful you are!" Then comes the crimson: the married woman who falls in love with another. The crimson will contrast with her naïveté, which can also be feigned. Like when she throws her engagement ring upon the Fountain of Forgetfulness. During the scene in the park, when the entire tragedy has been decided and the gates, through which she can still escape and go back, close with a crash, Mélisande could no doubt be white! White is just like black, an absolute color, actually the absence of color: absolute light or absolute darkness. Against a background of white, Pelléas's blood will be clearly visible. And in the last act, just like in the first, yellow. The color of the greatest source of energy projected upon a dying woman—anguish and the sun.

The actors will perform in half masks covering the forehead, eyes, and nose. Two male singers and one female, with a few textual modifications, can cover all seven characters without disorienting the viewer.

Berta lies in the grass beneath a tree while Rudi rehearses the love scene with a pair of singers. It's not dark, not even twilight, and the sun beats down on the garden. At a thousand meters above sea level, it is never very hot, and beneath the azure sky, which has become their rehearsal room, it is quite pleasant.

The darkness is meant symbollically anyway, thinks Berta.

Pelléas passionately exclaims, "Come, come, my heart beats madly, up to my very throat. Listen! Listen! My heart is almost strangling me. . . . Come!" And after a kiss, as from the pinnacle of a tall wave, he sings in a single tone, wonderstruck: "Oh, how beautiful it is in the darkness."

How beautiful it must be there.

Pelléas and Mélisande beneath the azure sky are trying to conjure up a stylized love embrace. It's more difficult than expected. The director is talking about the passion they must express in a single gesture. Not like that, says Rudi. That's too banal. Try something else. And he blushes at the same time.

Both Pelléas and Mélisande are crimson. But they don't give up.
Rudi looks over desperately at Berta, who is looking on from
her seat on the grass and starting to laugh. A moment later,
everyone is squirming. Oh God, says Ingrid/Mélisande wiping
away tears, it's embarrassing how innocent we are.

They plan the premiere for the twenty-sixth of August. The
invitations are printed up and sent out. The only thing left to
do is put together the performance, but it keeps breaking down
and unraveling for some reason.

Fortunately, the magnificent weather holds. Tents have
already been set up in the garden, and the young people are
relocating there to free up rooms in the villa for guests from
Vienna. Several artist acquaintances of Mrs. Meyer show up;
even the painter K. accepted the invitation. After two serious
injuries and long stays in the hospital, he has been exempted
from military service.

At first, his interest in the children's opera, as she calls it,
surprises Mrs. Meyer. After a brief consultation with Professor Kurz, an authority on Viennese love affairs, however, she
understands that the painter K. is most likely not attracted
by a desire for their company but, rather, by the idea that he
would have the chance to breathe the same air as his beloved
for a few days. His Immortal One, as the professor says. Several days ago, she departed for her home in Breitenstein with
a new lover, the poet Mendel from Prague. Otherwise, the
painter K. knows her house well; he had an opportunity to
paint some sort of snake for her above the fireplace. It is said
to be stunning.

Berta and her classmates would most like to pack up everything—the scenery, the costumes and masks—and slink off
somewhere. The idea that the renowned painter K. would be

a witness to their holiday diversion is unbearable. All of their creative achievements, which they were so proud of until now, virtually dissolve before their very eyes. Suddenly, they see them from the outside, and they appear dreadful.

Three days before the premiere, everyone is so nervous that Mrs. Meyer packs up enough food for the entire day and sends them off on an excursion to the mountains to clear their heads a little. She even sends Professor Kurz along with them. At least she'll have a break from him.

From the Semmering train station, they walk along the tracks to the Wolfsberg station and from there climb to the Doppelreiterwarte peak. It's hot and the hill wears them out. Especially Professor Kurz, who recalls with regret the agreeable and smoky comfort of the Viennese cafés, and the water from his canteen is not sufficient to revitalize him. They emerge from the evergreen forest onto a meadow blanketed with bluebells, lilies of the valley, and cyclamen. After they pause to refresh themselves, they continue up to a spot where they can look down onto the countryside.

Along the narrow ribbon of rail tracks from Klamm, their destination, a lone locomotive appears, racing toward them through clouds of steam. Like a nimble, well-fed rat it disappears into the cliff side with a whistle and then emerges a little farther on. It crosses the deep chasm along a viaduct, climbs the hill, passes through the mountain, and appears on another bridge on the other side. From here, you can make out three tunnels and two viaducts, according to Berta's count.

The railroad surmounts the differences in altitude in serpentine switchback turns, but they go straight, across Red Mountain to Breitenstein and, from there, along the rails to Klamm. Here they split up. Part of the group, led by Professor Kurz, sets off to find a pub. The other, which includes Rudi and Berta, go off to investigate the castle ruins on the cliff above the village.

Rudi and Berta hang back from the others and converse. Only when they run out of breath do they realize how marvelous the countryside is, but then something occurs to them and they return again to their stirring and somber meditations.

It's a play about light and darkness, says Rudi. As well as the ambivalence of guilt. Each is guilty in his own way and each is a victim: Mélisande, Pelléas, and Goulaud. For me, the sentence that expresses the play's essence is Goulaud's: *"Les enfants, ne jouez pas ainsi dans la obscurité."* Children, don't play in darkness. For in darkness, the erotic comes in contact with death.

The origin of tragedy lies in woman. Who is Mélisande? An unknown woman he discovers in the forest. Misfortune with the innocent face of a child lying in ambush for a man when he least expects it. She reveals nothing about herself, claiming simply that she was wronged. By whom? asks Goulaud. By everyone, she replies, everyone. But what if it's the other way around? What if she is the wrongdoer? Mélisande, even to herself, is an inscrutable conundrum. Finally, death will take them: her, the husband, and the lover. But the truth remains hidden. Or perhaps there is no truth. What if Goulaud only imagines there must be some sort of truth where there is actually only fog and haze?

Berta protests: No, Mélisande is not guilty. Goulaud is to blame for everything. He wanted to own her, but he didn't understand her. He wanted to tie her down like a rare, exotic bird. Her love for Pelléas is merely an escape. Why does Rudi, like all men today, demonize women this way? It's stupid. Look at me, says Berta. You think there's something dangerous in me?

Not in you, says Rudi. Which offends her.

The castle is much less interesting up close than from afar. They compete to see who makes it down first.

In the garden of the Castle Pub, the rest of the group are glutting themselves with bread and cheese washed down with beer. Professor Kurz, feeling somewhat better now, is merrily smoking away and calculating how many kilometers they must have covered. He doesn't leave out an inch of the trip, generously rounds it up, and in his calculations the excursion acquires respectable dimensions. Finally, he multiplies the result by two and is suddenly alarmed: Couldn't they take the train back to Semmering? Normally, this wouldn't be a problem, says the innkeeper, but hasn't the gentleman noticed there's a war on? I've heard something along those lines, grumbles the professor. And he fixes his eyes sadly on his lower extremities, as if trying to estimate how much longer they will hold out.

In the end, the painter K. did not come, and those who did show up made up their minds to enjoy themselves. The night was warmer than expected at the end of August; the torches and candles burned with a serene flame, illuminating the stage, along with the moon, which added to the magnificence. The musicians and singers made a minimum number of mistakes; the costume and scene changes went better than during the dress rehearsal, and afterward a supper was served on the terrace, from which one could not tell there was a war on.

After midnight, they dance. The large drawing room has already been cleared out beforehand in case it started to rain and they were compelled to perform inside. Students and friends of Mrs. Meyer take turns at the piano. Some couples dance on the terrace, then continue in the garden, disappearing among the larches. Berta does not dance. She has always felt that dancing was invented for other people, not her. The two or three experiences she had were so embarrassing that she blushes just thinking about it. Primarily, she's too small. Her legs are short. Certainly even people with short legs can dance, but it's never as nice as when Maja or Rudi glide across the parquet—slender, tall, fleet of foot, just like their mother, marvelous in her light gown with bared shoulders. The dancer looks perfect when he thinks he is, muses Berta. And I feel like an ungainly, plump puppy. She laughs. She has had some wine and isn't used to it. She sits on the terrace at the table where they had supper, with abandoned glasses, bottles, and bowls of fruit. The candles flicker. One half of the long table is bathed in light emanating from the living room; the other lies in darkness. Berta props her elbows on the table and rests her slightly heavy head on her hands. She has a vague feeling she is invisible.

Would you like some more? She's apparently not alone at the table; someone sits at the other end, shrouded in darkness. Berta sees the red end of a cigarette and notices the reflection of a glass lifted to lips; then the man reaches out for an unfinished bottle and Berta catches sight of his face. At first, it reminds her of a cat.

I'm twenty years old, he says as he finishes pouring. And you?

Berta assumes he's talking to her, since there's no one else here. Eighteen, she says, why?

I'm still a boy, he says. But I feel eighty years old. I look at them; some of them I knew before. Rudi, Maja, Ingrid, I don't know who else. Before. You know, it's strange. For a year, every day, it's been a matter of life and death, and you think only about how to survive. You have within yourself an enormous desire to live. You dream about what you would do if you could, and then when everything is over, you see that you really don't want to live at all. Everywhere you're a stranger. Emptiness peers out at you from behind everything. Everything seems senseless, and you suffer from a terrible feeling of guilt for something you could have had absolutely no influence on. You don't understand what other people say, why they do the things they do. For example, the opera you put so much into. Why? It's just a dead ornament. Nothing will change; nothing will be affected. It's a stupid piece. Sentimental and cloying. False. What is it actually about anyway? Jealousy. People write plays about that? I don't understand it. I stopped understanding. When you see a shredded body and smell the stench, you can't go back to Maeterlinck. But at the same time, between this sentimental slop, which you call symbolism, and murder, which I had to commit, there is a clear connection. Sentimentality goes hand in hand with cruelty. The person who kills because his female went off with someone else is the same as the person who murders for a piece of land, the right to self-determination, or a piece of food. And people are moved by it. Great thoughts, art, literature—what's it all for if man is still an animal at heart? No, not an animal. Animals are innocent. But we have a schism within. The head has no idea what goes on in the heart. And the gut. It doesn't want to know. Perhaps you know what I mean? Have you read Freud? What are you looking at? Rudi dancing with his sister? They look marvelous, don't they? Elegance . . . the mask of emptiness. And their mother, who has to take drugs because she's overly sensitive. People like her have to drug themselves, or else they would die from stabs of conscience. Or from emptiness. People die from emptiness nowadays. But you love them. Even this luxury, this would-be carefree atmosphere. You don't belong here, one can see that, but you like it.

You're right, they're beautiful. Rudi and Maja. "O sister! So still the golden day ends." Trakl wrote that. He also loved his sister. He went to war. And then shot his brains out.

The man almost shouts the last sentence.

Berta recoils. What does this person want from her? Why is he tormenting her?

Now he gets up and crosses the terrace with a wobbly step. He halts at the door frame, looks at the dancers, and Berta looks at him. He's slender, not too tall. Light red hair, a snub nose and somewhat slanted eyes. He's really still a boy. He turns his head to Berta and smiles. Lovely, as if the one in the dark were not he.

Perhaps we could live, he says. But we would have to invent something completely new, don't you agree?

Winter came early this year. The first snow fell at the end of October and blanketed the trees even as the branches held on to the last of their colored leaves. Crows arrived and their caws reminded one of a carrion field. A wolf wandered into Vienna from the Slovak mountains. No one has seen it, but at night they can hear it howling, and they've discovered the gnawed remains of stray dogs in several parks and cemeteries.

The monarchy has collapsed and a republic been declared. In the squares, people were marching for socialism, communism, nationalization, abortion, and cremation. Deserting soldiers and veterans formed Red Guard units, which, under the leadership of the journalist Hush and the poet Mendel, attacked and fired a few shots at the Austrian Parliament building and then the editorial offices of the *Viennese Herald*. The newspaper surrendered without a fight, and the editors agreed that the paper would be red. A special commando unit was established to tear off the white strip from all red-and-white Austrian flags, and there were so many strikes going on that the Socialist Party didn't even have time to write up proclamations.

Vienna was being killed off by the Spanish flu, and it was not safe on the streets at night.

We are participants in the painful birth of the New Man, the literary critic Mucke preached in the Café Central; shortly thereafter, he slipped out and headed for home. And never came back. The revolution assisted the virus, and the infection spread easily throughout the demonstrating crowds.

The Communist Party of Austria was established.

Under the pressure of events, the premier offered the Socialists participation in government, which they accepted. The Communists were shouting something about the historical moment, but their membership base wasn't important: a couple of artists and beggars. Even the flu was worn down. Whoever got infected now had a chance of survival. Its end did not come, however, until the winter frosts.

> *Who is Berta Altmann? Who is the I that is asking? Is it really possible to suddenly cease to exist? What does it mean that I survived while they are dead? How can I believe it? How can I accept it? Does some kind of soul really exist? Or is there only darkness and decay after death? I am alive and they are dead. Their beloved bodies—a convocation of worms.*
>
> *Oh God, whom does not exist! God, in which I long to believe at moments such as this! Where can I turn? What can I lean on? How can I bear this loneliness?*
>
> *The most difficult word: forever. And—nevermore.*

The model never stops moving, quickly or slowly, according to the rhythm the teacher beats out on the drum. Snowflakes descend on the glass roof of the studio, forming tiny drifts, melting, and sliding down due to the warmth from inside. The blue glow of the evening outside, the fireplace crackling within. Vienna is languishing from a shortage of wood, but here, because of the naked models, they must have heat.

That's the main reason evening drawing classes are so popular this year. The students come to get warm, say the professors. They envy the success of the new teacher, Meinlich, who was accepted from the Academy of Applied Arts in September to replace the late drawing professor Janecek.

A wave of enthusiasm swept through the students during the first few weeks of the school year, primarily directed at this young man wearing wire-rimmed spectacles.

Almost none of the professors can make sense of the enchantment that has possessed their charges. The students work with much greater diligence and overflow with ideas, but they're also unruly. They want to do everything their own way and they're brimming with bewildering ideas, which they could not have come up with themselves. They insist that each lesson begin with a ridiculous ten-minute breathing exercise, which is supposed to help initiate the flow of the subconscious and free the creative powers.

A naked man on a wooden platform in the middle of the room halts at Meinlich's signal, drapes a blanket over his shoulders, and sits down to rest. Berta drops her charcoal and waves her hand, which is already starting to hurt. She's here for the first time after a long illness. She doesn't know how to draw a moving body or even what the drum and rhythmic breathing of the students are supposed to mean. She also doesn't understand the religious silence of the students that sets in at the beginning of class when the teacher enters and starts speaking in a soft, indistinct voice. She understands nothing, but she doesn't care; she views events from outside, armored in her sorrow. She was afraid to go back to school, where she wouldn't find Maja. And now she's here, surrounded by familiar and unfamiliar faces; she's indifferent to them. She sits and holds her scratchings on her lap.

Meinlich walks among the students and examines their work. Here and there he injects a word or adds a line with a piece of charcoal, illuminating the drawing from another angle. When he halts by her side, Berta blushes: I'm here for the first time, she says.

Don't think, says Meinlich. Follow the curve of your breath, and with your hand the movement of the model.

From a distance, he looks like a boy, but up close he doesn't appear so young; he's definitely over thirty. When he smiles, wrinkles gather beneath his round spectacles. Something in the timbre of his voice or in the way he speaks produces a feeling of tranquillity in the listener, as if he were being absorbed by a warm, clear center. Later, his enemies will rename him the Snake Charmer and mock him, but Berta, just like her classmates, will succumb to him.

The snow is still falling.

At the end of the hour, most of the students pack up their things and, after respectfully saying good-bye to Meinlich, depart in groups of twos and threes. Berta packs up her drawing supplies and sketchbook in her leather satchel but is in no hurry to leave. She doesn't look forward to going back out into the chilly darkness. She's not the only one who's remained behind. A circle of five boys and girls has formed around the teacher, and they're trying to talk him into something. Apparently, they've acquired his consent and are merrily moving toward the door. When they pass Berta, who is still sitting lost in thought, one of them stops beside her and says, We're going on a walk with Robert. Want to come? It's a little cold, but Robert doesn't go to cafés.

She recognizes that voice.

A darkened terrace; inside, bright chandeliers and the faces of her friends. Red wine, in connection with something unpleasant. And then he shot his brains out!

Did you hear me?

She looks up, says, Do you know they're dead? Maja and Rudi?

Just pronouncing their names makes her eyes well with tears.

Come with us, he says, and picks up her bag. Just come.

They exit the school and turn left toward the city park. The snowstorm has just let up. They are the first people to leave their tracks on the clean surface. Someone suggests they make a snow statue. They work together in silence. Some sort of headless, bulky, recumbent woman emerges. Meinlich is happy as a child, like one of them. His presence arouses a sense of happiness in them. Disproportionate to external circumstances, as Berta later realized.

On the cover page of the complete works of Trakl's poems from 1918, which Berta entrusted to Kristýna in the depository, along with her other books, the fading dedication reads:

An Schwester Max, Weinacht 1918.

After the title of one of the poems, someone—Kristýna always assumed it was the donor—wrote an exclamation point and underlined the last quatrain.

Klage!
Schlaf und Tod, die duster Adler
Umrauschen nachtlang dieses Haupt:
Des Menschen goldnes Bildnis
Verschlänge die eisige Woge
Der Ewigkeit. An schaurigen Riffen
Zerschellt der purpurne Leib
Und es klagt die dunkle Stimme
Über dem Meer.

Schwester stürmischer Schwermut
Sieh ein ängstlicher Kahn versinkt
Unter Sternen,
Dem schweigenden Antlitz der Nacht.[2]

Beneath the poem is written in Berta's hand *Ich liebe Max.*

They became inseparable. Together they floundered through the anxieties of winter and together they greet the spring. They have ventured outside the city to the river. The young leaves are budding on the trees, the forest on the opposite bank is a translucent green, and the sun is slowly dissolving the morning fog. The ground is still cold, but there's a feeling of downy softness. And relief.

Suffering is unnecessary, thinks Max. Pain belongs to the old, and the old to the past. We are building new cities full of light and gardens, where people will learn to be happy and free. The colors of our paintings will introduce love into people's hearts. In the new society, without coercion, without jealousy, we will share our art and our life.

Berta bends down for a nicely formed branch. She turns it over and thrusts it into the soft earth. It's a bird.

A gryphon? asks Max.

Berta nods.

They reach the southern slope, which the sun has already managed to dry.

Berta turns around several times, closes her eyes, and plops down on the grass.

I would like to go to Italy, she says.

Let's go. Max nods. He feels the grass with his hand and only then sits down. Today for the first time he is wearing his light trousers.

Berta laughs out loud.

What are you laughing at?

You're so careful.

The sun spreads in all directions upon the surface of the water, lightly stirred by the wind, and suffuses their eyes with radiance.

Berta spreads her arms wide and cries out like a hawk.

They breakfast on sandwiches Berta has brought along from home, wash them down with bottled water, and then take a walk along the river. The sun is beginning to burn. Max makes a little hat out of his handkerchief and covers his head. His sensitive white skin is beginning to redden, and his freckles are breaking out.

Sometime after noon, they arrive at the ferry, next to which is a pub and beer garden. They order cold beer and sit beneath a chestnut tree, which still has not begun to cast a proper shadow. Then they talk about what they always talk about when they're together, in one way or another.

Robert is leaving for Weimar in the fall, says Max. That's certain. They're opening a brand-new school there, a community, rather, founded on the principle of medieval artistic guilds. The architect Czerny is the director. The city gave him part of the building of an academy there and also promised some sort of government subsidies if it becomes successful. You see, there are plans to make Weimar the capital of a sort of European Republic of the Spirit. With Goethe in mind. Robert will teach the compulsory introductory course, and only then will the students decide which trade or art they want to devote themselves to. There, he will have a much greater influence on things. To create, meditate, eat, and relax in common—do you realize what that would mean? An enormous artistic and spiritual leap forward. He said we should go with him. The two of us, Ludwig and Mário. Apparently, he hasn't told anyone else about it. He believes we are the most prepared, and we would be able to support him in the new environment. He said he already has an agreement with the school. We can go with him, and it wouldn't be any more expensive than studying in Vienna.

Berta is excited. They would leave this place, go far away from the memories, the family house, from everything that hurts too much. Begin a new life. With new friends, they would create and work on a new, better world.

We'll never come back, says Berta.

Her erstwhile dream, but with Max.

She remembers something: Did you know that Czerny's former wife married Mendel the poet?

You know those things don't interest me, retorts Max. He's not into gossip.

They return by the same path. The beer and sun have worn them out, and they walk in silence. The slope on which they ate their breakfast is soft and warm in the late-afternoon light. Berta sprawls out among the daisies and dandelions; Max remains sitting, then lights up a cigarette and smokes, avidly, as he learned to in the trenches, gazing at the tip of the cigarette consuming itself.

Berta looks up into the azure sky mounting above her and pulling her up as if she were gazing into the interior of a cathedral. Perhaps God is not dead, she thinks. That boundless azure is God.

As if confirming her thoughts, a bird of prey cries out far above them in the air.

Max turns his head: a hawk.

They look at each other and feel a little ashamed. It's the first time they've seen each other like this, divested of sweaters and coats, and they seem naked to each other.

Berta, naturally dark, has turned golden in the sun. Her short, dark brown hair is disheveled and falls across her tanned face. She looks pretty, fresh, in a short-sleeved white blouse and brown knit vest with a corduroy skirt reaching above her ankles. Her eyes, which are dark in the city, have suddenly turned green. Spring eyes, thinks Max.

All of a sudden, it occurs to him that Berta is a young woman and he a young man. It's the first time since the war he's sensed this. He feels like kissing her.

She stares at him from behind the curtain of her lashes. She might not even be breathing.

Max gazes at the river and then the sun as it sinks into the forest.

It's late, he says. We should be heading back.

With other girls he kissed, he felt different from the way he does with Berta. This confuses him. He feels relaxed around her, like with a man. Again he looks at her furtively and is again surprised: It's as if he were seeing her for the first time. But the moment for a kiss has passed. The girl's gaze is once again fixed above.

Sometimes, whispers Berta, I have the feeling they're with us, Maja and Rudi. And they're asking us to be happy for them.

We will be, says Max. Perhaps somewhat absently, because he cannot free himself from the astonishing realization that his best friend is a girl. He feels almost deceived.

Chapter 3

Weimar

He put away his old name along with his civilian clothes. Now he is Theodor Noor.

He spent the summer at Lake Constance in the home of his spiritual master and received from him the equivalent of an ordination. No, nobody demanded he don a red robe and shave his head; one could not even recognize many of the adherents of the Teaching among the commoners. But Meinlich doesn't do anything halfway. The Arabic Al-Noor means spiritual light. He came up with this new name himself.

Through long fasting, he brought himself into a state of heightened sensitivity; his enemies would have called it nervous irritation. He lost weight and his eyes grew wider behind his spectacles. But asceticism has not reduced his strength. On the contrary. He is eliminating all obstacles to allow his spiritual energy to flow freely. By obstacle—in addition to superfluous thoughts—he means primarily the body.

Light and darkness. The God of good and the God of evil. Art is white, war black. The spirit strives upward, matter downward, the spirit toward the center, matter away from it. Only enlightened matter conforms to the injunctions of the spirit, the laws of creation, the movement upward and forward.

The time of the old world has come to an end; a new era is

dawning. Bloody catastrophes were necessary for the New Man to arise, the prophet of a new kind of spirituality: Art.

For the first six months in Weimar, they spend time only with each other. There are fewer than twenty students of various ages. Every one of them has encountered war and death. They seem uncertain. The entirety of venerable, ritualized society has collapsed and disintegrated before their eyes like a rotten dinghy. They must push on further, alone, with fierce waves and an empty horizon ahead. They cleave to one another and to Meinlich. The architect Czerny is burdened with concerns of the organization and financing of the school—Meinlich has a free hand. Of the five teachers, three of them will turn to the Teaching; among the students, Berta, Max, Mário, and Ludwig will form the heart of the group of devotees that will attract others. They adore Meinlich. Only he holds the answers to all their questions; to him, all secrets have been revealed, from the creation of the world to reincarnation. He demands of them cleanliness of body and mind; he wants them to forgo meat and to fast, meditate, and perform breathing exercises. It cleanses their senses and sharpens their instincts. He wants them to develop their intuition, to play like children, and discover within themselves once again the genius of childhood. The artist must posses the naive eye and heart of a child, he says. Everything is allowed in his classes, even tears.

He shows them the way to curiosity. They seek out new materials, new forms, unusual combinations. New impulses. They search for them in attics, basements, kitchens, junkyards—everywhere miracles lie in wait.

Noor, whom his previous students are allowed to call Robert, doesn't so much correct them as help them not go astray. He guides them toward enchanting discoveries on the path to gradual liberation, the search for one's own individuality and expression.

Berta continues her studies in the textile workshop. Max has decided to abandon painting for architecture, the field placed highest in the hierarchy of the school's values, the synthesis of all the arts, the copestone, the roofing, and the unifying principle simultaneously.

I've decided not to bother with dates.

What is abstraction? The purest, most truthful essence, the foundation of the object. One must reduce and discard everything extraneous, illusory, ephemeral, changeable until only the essential remains: the principle. Color, line, form. Senses deform. Memory deforms. We must penetrate to the heart, the essence, which is singular and unchanging. This essence is Truth. We do not find it through reason, but through insight, intuition. But first it is necessary to divest oneself of all the ballast that entire centuries have deposited within the human soul. All superstitions, sentimentality, false ideas, enslavement. Everything society has inculcated in us.
The foundation we seek is the same for everyone.

We paint light. We break it down into the spectrum, refract it through crystal. We compel the invisible to appear. Dematerialize the world. How does one paint light?
(And silence. How does one paint birdsong?)

I don't have a lot of time for writing; something's always happening. And when things are happening, you can't write them down. Everything is in motion, internal

alteration is essential. Everything is intensive. The shar-
ing, the exchange of ideas and impressions. Perpetual
work. Sometimes it's too much, and I feel I am emptying
myself unduly. After long conversations, I'm exhausted.
What do we talk about all the time? Mostly art, of
course: What it is, exactly? What is its task in the mod-
ern world? How can we change the world through art?
What needs to be changed? The greatest problem appears
to be that after we in the West abandoned our belief in
the Christian God, we lack a unifying idea. This is what
art could be.

Today Czerny told us our school is like a laboratory
in which we are developing a model of the future society.
Robert corrected him: not a society, a spirituality. Czerny
replied that what makes a society a society is precisely a
unified manner of spirituality.

Debates about the other reality: In addition to the pri-
mary reality that tangibly surrounds us is another real-
ity, the world of the human soul. But this other reality
is a kind of foundation shaping the primary reality. We
know very little about it. We must map the world of the
soul, with all its shadowy corners and points of illumi-
nation. But without the help of images borrowed from
the external world. That's how it used to be, but that's
not what we want! We do not seek to illustrate, but,
rather, to materialize directly what truly is. Instead of a
sad countryside, depict sadness itself.

Images of the soul must issue from the material of the
soul, nowhere else. To perceive directly! To dissolve the
unnecessary. To again tread the path of the art of paint-
ing, from the first spatters and strokes of paint. Cavemen

did not reproduce animals in drawings; they captured their immediate essence.

(The proximity of painting and magic.)

Rediscover the meaning of art.

In school, everyone thinks Max and I are seeing each other. Today my classmate V. let it slip. She's originally from Russia, and her parents fled before the revolution. I asked her why. Wouldn't it have been more interesting to stay? She said it might have been interesting, but only until the Bolsheviks shot them. She said I couldn't imagine it, and not even the Russians understand what's going on at the moment in Russia.

I think émigrés exaggerate things to justify their flight. Max and I are interested in communism. Max even said that if he wasn't so traumatized by the war, he might go fight in Russia. For the Reds, of course. As far as going out with each other, we once talked about the possibility with Robert, but in the end we decided not to overburden our relationship. Robert said that if we embarked on experiments with our bodies when we were still imperfect, he could not take responsibility for our further spiritual development. We gave him our word.

I read Kandinsky: He describes the Good as the Creative Spirit, a movement forward and upward, a white ray. Evil is matter, a black hand standing in the way of the white ray, holding it back.

All the things that must be banished: decoration, aestheticization (the pursuit of beauty), imitation. Internal disingenuousness and any kind of artificial evocation of emotion. Habitual associations, habitual ways of seeing. What's that? Perspective perhaps? The conviction that an object in the foreground must be larger than one in the background. Perspective is actually a kind of violence we commit on our perception. It is necessary to paint the way we perceive, the way we feel, not the way we think we think (geometrically). Space and time are subjective; the universe is subjective. We discover it within ourselves and not beyond ourselves. Painting is experimentation, attempts to cognize the truth about ourselves and the universe.

Today Czerny had a talk with us. Apparently, those of us around Robert are isolating ourselves from the rest and behaving like a sect. What nonsense! He repeated once again that we must function like a democratic, model collective. If we succeed, it will prove that a better world can actually be created from human material. That's why it's so important. Another debate about the laboratory and the New Man.

Our greatest task, the task of our times, is the creation of a new form that will fully express this period, just as previous periods were expressed by their own forms. But can such a form be created deliberately? Doesn't it emerge from somewhere unfamiliar and of its own, instinctively— organically? That's possible. We lack a unifying principle, some sort of basis. It's as if everything were falling apart in our very hands.

It's a matter of finding the one unifying thing! Some kind of order.

Robert wants us to discover original joy within ourselves, the original naïveté of perception. It's like peeling an onion. We peel back layer after layer, beginning with our childhood, everything our parents, our society, our schools hammered into us, out of goodwill or ill. Things we consider positive are even more dangerous, says Robert. The negative things will fall away of themselves. The process he calls an absolute cutting off. He has his own methods, but the basic idea derives from Eastern thought. Robert claims that the state of original joy is a return to the immediacy of childhood. Nothing must come between you and the world, he says. You and the world. You and the world. What do you hear? What do you feel? What genuinely interests you about the world? Only through this authenticity will your art attain power. It will penetrate the human soul like a knife. In its simplicity and transparency, it will be as sharp as the facet edge of a crystal.

Combinations of contrasting materials. Feathers and stone. Feathers and metal. Wool and glass. Wood and metal. The surprise of contradictory perceptions allows us to discover new possibilities of expression. The abundance of sensual perceptions: arousing the sense organs. Inexhaustible diversity.

I sense Max becoming more distant; he spends much more time with students who arrived halfway through the school year. I also try to open up and make new friends. Max says we're too closed off and involved in each other, that we must destroy our mutual haven (our prison) and lay ourselves open to new influences. Let ourselves be inspired by the collective. So I open myself up.

What is the most important thing in creation? To be faithful to oneself, faithful to the feeling I have at that instant and which I externalize. To undertake the entire voyage, to experience with my entire body, not just my mind. The Chinese say that when painting, the heart and hand must be one. Let yourself be absorbed!

But: If my ego does not participate in the creation, who is actually creating? Robert says it's God, some higher power, the good (the white ray). Let a higher power operate through you. Here artistic creation is identical to spiritual practice. I merely assist and provide the material. I must admit I've experienced this feeling only twice. Once when I was little and then here, in Weimar, during one of Robert's classes. Exaltation—ecstasy. Suddenly, you have no doubts. You know exactly what comes next; the path reveals itself. But all it takes is one false step, broken concentration, faulty motivation (issuing from the ego and not the superego), and the creative thread is rent; what was clear before goes dark.

28 February 1920
Today Max and I had a real fight. It was about whether painting must subordinate itself to architecture. I think it doesn't; Max thinks it does. He says that in the new art, pictures will be painted directly onto a clearly defined space. He says painting by itself is egocentric and has a disruptive effect. In the new art, all elements must be subordinated to a single whole. A whole that is designed and directed by a single authority—the architect. Everything must function according to predetermined criteria and intents.

This seems somewhat overstated. I had to laugh when I imagined pictures being painted to order in precisely determined colors and sizes. Max said I shouldn't laugh, this was very real, and it would be real very soon. Paintings of the future will have a precisely calculated effect. The new artist would not waste time expressing his own limited, individualistic emotions, but, rather, devote himself to investigating the effects of individual colors and shapes, so he can capture them and thereby evoke the common emotions of the greatest number of people. Typical emotions. The painter will produce paintings, and inexpensive copies will be printed so that everybody can have one. That is the future, said Max, and not the romantic nonsense you envision.

How does he know what I envision? We haven't had a proper talk for at least a month, and now he comes to argue. I was surprised. Our opinions are suddenly entirely at odds and differ completely from those we both used to profess and which brought us to Weimar with Robert.

I asked him why he had changed so suddenly and so completely. He said he realized that our searching with Meinlich wasn't leading anywhere, and we would keep spinning in a circle because we would never discover the unifying principle and foundation of everything through some childish self-examination and purification. The truth is not going to fall out of the sky. We have to invent it with our minds. What genuinely benefits mankind? Not mystification, but organization, science, technology, and progress. And this is what art must subordinate itself to. Everything that smacks of individualism is reactionary and harmful, including the Teaching.

It appears he's not the only one in the school to hold

such opinions. When I wanted to talk with Robert about it, he got angry.

8 March 1920

Last night something really strange happened and I don't know what to think about it. Max asked me to remain in the workshop until everyone else left. He said he wanted to apologize. It was dark outside and snowing, even though it's already March. The snowflakes on the windowpanes reminded me of the night we built a snow statue in the park. I said this to Max. Is it possible that only a year and four months has passed since Maja's and Rudi's deaths? We sat together in the dark and talked. Max explained why he grew angry with me; apparently, he feels frustrated. He thinks we're marching in place and wasting time. Lately he's become exceptionally impatient. He wants to break through. Soon he'll be twenty-four; other men his age are building their careers, and what is he doing? Sitting and meditating. Apparently, he's suddenly felt the necessity for speed, adventure, and the churchlike atmosphere around Robert depresses him. He's angry at Robert. I'm no longer certain of anything, he kept repeating, but I know that something is slipping away, and I want to capture it before it's too late.

Then he asked me if I wanted to go away with him to Berlin at once and try to break through on our own. I promised to think about it. He said, Make up your mind quickly.

Then we left the workshop together. Max wanted to accompany me all the way home. Suddenly, when standing in front of the door, he kissed me and said he wanted to come upstairs. I had no idea this was coming, and I

started to stammer something. I think I used Vera as an
excuse. Max didn't insist. He just said, Fine. And left.

I don't even remember how I got up the stairs and
unlocked the door. I was in shock. I changed into my
pajamas, but I couldn't get to sleep. The sky was white. I
sat on the windowsill and smoked, behind the glass a sparkling space. Something drew close to me; just reach out
your hand. At one point I opened the window; the moon
peeped out between ribbons of clouds. I fell asleep as it
was already getting light. I woke up again an hour later.
Afraid that I'd overslept and missed something important.
I was gripped with excitement. What's next?

10 April 1920
And then nothing. Max pretends nothing happened, and
a month has gone by already (a dreadful month). Apparently, it was a momentary lapse (ha-ha). I cry. You are
so stupid, Berta! Max avoids me, and I can't get up the
courage to ask him what it was supposed to mean. I'm not
even sure it actually happened.

15 April 1920
Today Robert brought to class a slide of a weeping
Madonna by Grünewald. We were supposed to express the
essence of the work with a single curved line. After we
had been working for about half an hour, Robert suddenly leaped up and started shouting at us, saying we were
unemotional and untalented blocks of wood. If we had
only an ounce of artistic sensitivity, we wouldn't befoul
our paper and nibble our pencils when face-to-face with
the purest expression of pain, but instead we would ourselves break down in tears. Then he ran out and slammed

*the door. I actually started crying, and someone, I think it
was Leo, said that Noor's nerves were starting to give out.*

The number of both students and teachers increased the second
semester, and a tension began to emerge within the school. The
professors are starting to complain: Noor's group behaves like a
closed sect, and Noor himself is acting like some kind of guru.
No decision is made without his consent. His students are
damaging the community with their individualism; they refuse
to submit to anything that doesn't conform to their internal
impulses, and they will accept no restrictions. They see every
well-intentioned piece of advice or request as an attack on their
person, and instruction is becoming progressively impossible.
Furthermore, their heads are filled with some kind of mysti-
cal nonsense. Noor invites guests to his classes who have nothing to do with the school. Every itinerant prophet, messiah, or
vagabond visionary—something with which postwar Germany
abounds—finds the door to his classroom open.

In the circular room where the entire school gathers for
meetings, Czerny harangues the students: Our efforts are spiritual, but each of us cannot succeed by himself. Our ideal of
a communal work of art is like a Gothic cathedral on which
every anonymous artist carries out his task while strictly subordinated to the collective goal. What humanity is lacking today
is a single, universal, spiritual idea. It is our task, here, in this
community, to realize it through humble, collective work. Our
common work of art will become its crystallization and its
expression, precisely as a Gothic cathedral was the expression
of the idea of the Christian God. If the result is to be a residential home, it will be a home. If it is to be a factory, it will be a
factory. Let us be patient. We must allow it to mature slowly.
As Kandinsky, someone whom I hope to bring here one day,

wrote, necessity creates form. This necessity manifests itself in its own time, at its own moment, and it is up to us to be prepared for this moment. Work on yourselves under the guidance of your professors, improve your technique and sensitivity to such a degree that we might become the instrument of the idea as soon as it desires to assume its form. This is our great and unique task, our communal task to save humanity. But humility is needed.

When the director finishes, the students break out in applause. He speaks almost as well as Noor. The impression of his lecture is spoiled only by his civilian, somewhat bureaucratic exterior. Noor is sitting in his red robe, unmoving, like a statue of the Buddha. His eyes are closed and his thoughts seem elsewhere. But when the ovation subsides, when silence sets in and attention naturally transfers itself to him, Noor opens his eyes, looks around at the faces in the room, raises his right hand after the fashion of the prophets, and softly, as he usually speaks, says, Art does not serve. Art is sovereign. The artist is not a tool; the artist is sovereign. The individual is the beginning and the goal. The child within us. The genius within us. That is the good. That is the universal . . . the idea. No, our objective is not and cannot be the created object, but always the subject. Always only the subject. His is the salvation. The final product is of no importance; it is the path that matters. The creation of light, Ahura Mazda.

It takes the students a moment to digest his words, and then they break out in applause once again, this time louder. This is a challenge to which Czerny must reply: I founded this community as a vision of medieval artists' guilds and cooperatives. Working on a communal creation does not mean repudiating one's own autonomous person. On the contrary, it is the fruit of its full development. But it assumes respect for the communal goal, an understanding of its significance, the sharing of a single spirit, which the artist-laborer fulfills. It does not matter what we call this spirit.

The applause is weak. Noor again plunges into meditation and closes his eyes. The director decides to continue, to say even that which he originally wanted to avoid: It is also a question of the physical survival of the school. If we don't have the revenue for its operation, considerations of the interpretation of our spiritual mission are superfluous. We must acquire subsidies. And to acquire subsidies, we must defend our right to exist. This means we must produce something. Demonstrate results.

Silence, the students feel they've been assaulted. Noor raises his hand to signal his desire to speak. His voice quavers: The name of darkness is Anga Mainyu. He is the father of money and profit. We cannot join the side of evil! Our goal is to free ourselves, to banish from body and mind everything ponderous and dark. The child does not worry what he will eat on the morrow. If it is to be three leaves of cabbage, it is to be three leaves of cabbage. Let us not discuss money on these grounds!

Even the director appears upset: It must be discussed. I've done nothing else for the past year but concern myself with it. And I'm telling you it is necessary if we want to survive. We must organize an exhibition as soon as possible. Whoever does not want to cooperate, whoever wants to undermine and ruin our communal effort, should consider leaving the school. Even though it would be a loss for us all.

Noor jumps to his feet, completely forgetting any spiritual pretense:

Do you have someone particular in mind? he asks.

It would be a great loss for us all, repeats Czerny. This person is an excellent pedagogue and we need him.

Noor wraps his robe around him tightly, as if suddenly

struck by the cold. He exits the room, alone; his devotees are not courageous enough to stand up for him openly.

Noor renounces his function on the school board and theatrically refuses to participate in any decisions concerning its further direction. Soon, however, he is dealt another blow. At the beginning of the second year, Czerny makes his age-long plan a reality and invites to the school, as full-time professors, his friends from the Young Germany movement, Wassily Kandinsky and Paul Klee.

Max Jauner. Max Jauner. They were supposed to be together forever. Max Jauner. He promised they would be happy. They would leave for Berlin together and open a studio. Altmann—Jauner, Jauner—Altmann. Why give up on it? he said. How could cheerful Max empathize with Berta, who is dying, who is practically dead already, bled to death, lacerated by the agonizing pain he has caused her, Max Jauner. Max the cautious. Max the builder of a better world. Max the Communist, Max the architect. Berta no longer fits into his plans. Max with a handkerchief on his head. Departing Max. Beneath the serene May sky. Beneath trees suffused with sunlight. Max in the wind. How did you think it was going to be, Berta? You, too, are free. We were just friends, after all; that's the way you wanted it. We still are. Berta and Max. Nothing has changed in this respect. You can go with us if you want. Do you want to? Max, the generous one. What if she says yes?

I can't take it, Max Jauner. I cannot bear the pain, minute after minute. Each minute seeks to take my life. I'm sinking, Max Jauner. And the night remains silent.

A woman seduces him away, older and stronger than he is. She came to the school to dance; she's a dancer. A modern dancer. The movements she executes in these dances strike Berta as indecent. She fancied him among all the others.

Berta doesn't know how it happened; everything was organized and agreed upon without her. Suddenly, Max is standing before her, announcing he's getting married, leaving for Berlin, where his fiancée has her base, as she calls it. She travels a lot. She's famous. She's famous and wants to marry him. Of course he's going to continue his studies at the Berlin Academy.

Love is eminently simple, Max informs her.

His fiancée does not want it to get into the newspapers.

He's vexed Berta cannot be happy.

He'll write her soon.

Instead of going to school, Berta wanders outside the city, walks aimlessly until all but unconscious, until her body no longer perceives the fatigue and the pain in her chest, where it has closed itself off, not allowing her to breathe, benumbed. Only then does she go back home, fall into bed, and sleep. Nobody asks her anything. Jauner's sudden departure surprised everyone.

From one of her walks, Berta brings home a ginger-haired kitten. It was licking discarded peels by some trash bins. She names him Max.

Nostalgia, the grizzled sadness, drowns out the feelings of injustice and betrayal. Life plays out independently of her; she no longer belongs to it. Something has been interrupted that shouldn't have. Berta is forgetting who she was before.

Time frightens her most of all. Time. The days and nights she will have to get through, the monotonous series of hours that break down beneath the stress of the pain into interminable minutes, 1,440 minutes a day she must somehow get through, besides those she spends sleeping, and not go insane. Time is a prison. Her thoughts are a prison, her dependence on Max. She is pinned to her situation like an insect to a piece of cardboard.

Berta seeks relief wherever she can; she reads the Bible. The enumeration of names and prescriptions in the Old Testament calm her, as does the story of the sufferings of Jesus Christ. She reads at random, skips around; she doesn't have the patience. Only when something touches her especially deeply does she stop. Thus she winces over several sentences in the Gospel According to Luke, which mention Anna the Prophetess. The mysterious "daughter of Phanuel, of the tribe of Asher" takes hold of her imagination: "She was advanced in years and had lived with her husband seven years after her marriage, and then as a widow to the age of eighty-four. She never left the temple, serving night and day with fastings and prayers."

The unfamiliar face and figure of a woman closed off in a temple becomes for Berta a place of relief.

Berta begins to carve Saint Anne from stone. With the coarse grayish stone, she is no longer lost; she has something in her hands to hold on to. The stone replies to her in conversation, becomes a body to which, with great effort and cursed cumbrousness, she provides a gradually emerging form. The figure she is carving is her newly found countenance. And in some mysterious way perhaps the face of her dead mother, as well.

When Berta completes the statue, it is October. She feels exhausted, like after an illness, but also empty and light, and with this newly acquired lightness, she throws herself into the life of the school. She's suddenly everywhere; she has fun and works as much as two, two Bertas. She's always busy, filling herself with new things. She gets delirious, then crumbles, and at those moments she has the courage to think about it, she sees herself drifting away from herself, but she is not unhappy. Her dreadful pain has frozen over somewhere. There are days when she doesn't even think about Max.

Besides Meinlich, who has closed himself up in his Teaching and doesn't communicate even with his close friends, she is enchanted most of all by the quiet and kind Paul Klee. She goes to his studio, learns to translates her thoughts and feelings into graphic symbols, which she then weaves into tapestries, sews on pillows and covers.

One form continually repeats itself, becomes the basic element of all her compositions. It looks like a snail. An unending spiral winding in on itself.

Chamalam midliyee, grundulum paprio. Alehuja karnavalakulum. Tresepeti kuruptajlaa, mesli kusli farli daa. Oslekguslemrakhtipijaa funkulunkum herde rakh.

That's when he's in an expansive mood. But more often he is spare of word.

Theodor, hello.

Kurdum mek!

Do we have class today?

Kurdum mek!

Nice weather, isn't it?

Kundrum mek!

How do you feel?

Mek kurdum!

Or he doesn't reply at all, just shakes his head and places a finger to his lips. He hitches up his robe and skips a few dance steps in his bare feet, spins around on his own axis until he's dizzy, then bumps into things and starts laughing. He lies down on the grass, kicks his legs up in the air, and sings disconnected snatches of melody. Or he bares his behind at the school board.

Kurdum mek!

When the students come to class, they find him sitting on one of the tables, weaving wreathes from meadow flowers. Naked. He decorates his students with flowers and green leaves and forces them to dance while he gambols naked in front of them with a serious countenance.

He covers himself entirely in paint and prints himself on canvases and white walls, dozens of striding, lying, kneeling Meinlichs, marvelously colored, haloed Meinlichs. Isn't it beautiful? They are to undress and do the same.

Have you lost your mind?

Must you go all the way, Meinlich? We realize that you know full well you're not a child. You're not a child, Robert Meinlich; you're a pedagogue here and have responsibilities. You have to work here, Robert Meinlich; you cannot continue here like that. Feigning insanity and sticking your rump out at us! This is not amusing, Robert Meinlich. Do you know whom you have to thank for your ongoing presence here? Mr. Klee. He is standing up for you. But we will not heed his intercessions for long, not even out of decorum.

During the 1922–1923 school year, the postwar poverty in Germany reaches its peak. The value of money drops from hour to hour; those lucky enough to still receive a paycheck head with their suitcases stuffed with notes to the stores to do the shopping quickly, before the price of goods rises several fold. One shoelace costs as much as a shoe factory used to; a hundred dollars can purchase an entire residential street. The only ones who thrive are the crooks and the owners of nightclubs, where the burglarized and crestfallen try to forget.

The school is also burdened with financial difficulties, but the creative atmosphere is not affected at all. On the contrary: It's as if the chaos of inflation has suddenly unleashed all forces.

Everything imaginable becomes possible; all barriers fall in both art and sex. Every experiment is applauded as long as it's new. What once was, no longer is, or it's standing on its head. There's always something to celebrate. The wind pushes into the roof, a celebration of wind. It rains, a celebration of water. Carnivals become popular, and the masks go beyond all measure and limits of fantasy. The school has its own band. They call it jazz, but it's more like pandemonium and buffoonery; everyone pounds on whatever is at hand, from cowbells to chairs. There's also a special dance that goes with it, a complicated set of absurd gestures and capers, which instantly become fashionable and are performed at artists' gatherings throughout Germany. The world is reeling, each element wriggling in its own way, and enthroned at the center of all the confusion and contradictory movements is not God, but man who is gazing forward: into a joyous future that he will direct without prejudice and in his own way.

At the end of the 1923–1924 school year, the board is preparing its first major exhibition to present the work of its students to the German public. The main exhibit will be neither pictures nor sculptures, but a model of a furnished house for five young individuals. Participation is mandatory.

Theodor Noor condemns the path taken by the school; he is against selling students' work, the pursuit of results and success. It cripples the young, he says. We should be developing their personalities, providing them space in which to thrive freely and not forcing them into anything. We should not be making them into tradesmen who will soon be pandering to the tastes of manufacturers.

Most oppose him.

Noor is given immediate notice, and Berta decides to leave, as well. She feels she's learned enough at the school. But where is she supposed to go? Back to Vienna?

She writes to Max and receives an immediate answer. Come, writes Max. Berlin is fantastic. Things are definitely getting better, and the two of us must start working together, at last.

> *Parallel lines intersect in infinity. And the moon's averted face does not exist. The moon is a flat, smooth disk on the dome of the sky. The two of us together. I don't intend to concern myself with anything else. I don't want to construct a cold, geometrical world with no place for miracles. By force, with my reason. I want to be the creator of my own world, its inception and its culmination. To have the courage to achieve my truth! To live the way I must. Nobody else but me. But you were, are, and will be above and before me. I will surrender myself to you voluntarily. Here, take everything I have. Make of me a light and luminous offering. Pain cannot dwell within this lightness. I share you with no one else. I cannot steal from her something she never had.*

In 1934, when Kristýna met Berta, the Weimar school still existed. In a different city with a different director, but under the same name. Over the previous ten years, it had created the modern furniture design most in demand in Europe. With the motto Maximal Effect, Minimal Means, it had gone from cathedrals and the salvation of mankind to chairs, thinks Kristýna. Then the Nazis abolished the school. They hauled off the protesting students and expelled the foreigners from the country.

From everything Kristýna had read about the school and everything she'd heard from Berta, she could not say whether it had been such an asset for her friend as it might at first have seemed. Hadn't she lost her way in all the concepts and programs these important men had glutted her with? How obstinate she would have had to have been, despite everything, to paint what she genuinely gravitated toward: a bouquet of flowers, for example. At the school, they jeered at easels and painting from life. Later, they began to disdain even painting itself. From Noor's deification of talent, they went all the way to rejecting it entirely: For them, an artist was an oversensitive monkey. The studio, they called a "workshop," architecture a "construction," and in place of pictures, they championed advertising posters, and films instead of sculpture. Klee and Kandinsky remained at the school until the end, but somewhere out of the way; most of the students were engaged in designing new houses filled with new furniture for new people—who, over the course of time, turned out to be not so different from the old people. They preferred a different shape of lamp, but did they therefore manifest less inclination toward violence?

Berta herself claimed that the most valuable thing she had taken away from Weimar was the requirement of absolute freedom, the courage to create one's own life oneself, despite tradition.

Kristýna has not been able to work for several days, and it agonizes her. She's addicted to daily meditation, as she calls it. Sometimes it lasts two hours, other times three, and sometimes she just goes for a walk and doesn't draw a single line. Nevertheless, she has the feeling she's accomplished something. The quality of sight, the integration of contiguity with intuition, with creative energy. The long disuse of this ability, Kristýna has noticed, blocks access to it: ideas, fears, sometimes qualms, which, according to Kristýna, serve only as an excuse to do nothing. She has never stopped creating for a long period of time, not even when her son was little, not even when he was sick, not even when she had to work at the factory eight hours a day. She always found at least an hour a day. Work does her good. When she was drawing, painting, or putting together a collage, she was happy. Discontentment arose when she had finished one thing and not yet begun another.

She can't do any work because she keeps replaying in her head the filmmakers' visit from Israel. The conversation about Berta had upset Kristýna, stirred up within her a series of doubts and reproaches, questions to which she still has not found an answer. And time is getting shorter. She curses herself for agreeing to be filmed. She feels abused. And what's worse is that she cannot remember what she actually talked about. She knows only that she spoke for a long time. She had always sneered at people who babbled on television, as she called it. And now the same thing had happened to her. As soon as they pointed the camera at her, she lost control; her mind was eclipsed. She's certain she talked about things she'd promised she wouldn't, their great quarrel, for instance.

In 1940, Berta could have left for England, but she refused because that would have meant leaving her husband.

He can take care of himself, Kristýna told her. He'll get his papers and follow you over later.

She shook her head. He's my husband; I promised never to leave him. He's my responsibility

You are your primary responsibility, pleaded Kristýna. He's only half Jewish; he can save himself. And you're a Communist, after all!

Berta had to smile at that.

Why is he so important to you? You don't have any children, and you're not happy with him anyway!

Even now she winces when she recalls those words. They're one of the injuries she has afflicted in her life, injuries that accompany her everywhere like bothersome relatives. She'll take them with her to the grave even if those whom she hurt have long forgiven her, have forgotten them, or are dead. How could she have allowed herself to do that to Berta? She was so stupid; she knew nothing about life. As if she, with her all but infantile experiences, could understand why her friend was so reluctant to leave for England.

Her words frightened Berta, but she didn't let it show. She merely had this momentary wounded look in her eyes.

Kristýna vents a curse.

Back then, she had the feeling that Berta, fourteen years her senior, was more naive and defenseless than she was, and that she had to save her. She was so open to everything, so generous to everybody, she kept nothing for herself. Her devotion resembled resignation, and this irritated Kristýna. She thought Berta should behave more selfishly; only thus could she create the kind of work she was meant to. That alone was reason enough for her to leave. Her exhibition in England had been successful; there were people who could help her. She would survive, and not just survive: She could become a great artist, like she'd always longed to be. Instead, she chose the village, work in a textile shop, escalating slights, and finally deportation.

She had also recounted to them the story of the last night before Berta and her husband boarded the train to Terezín. The entire previous day, Kristýna helped them pack their suitcases. It was like a bad dream. Again and again they would take everything out, organize and weigh it, think about what they would really need in the camp and what they couldn't do without. Sometime around 2:00 A.M. everything was finally ready, and Berta said they should all go to sleep. At five, they had to get up again. They had already been living in an attic for the two months remaining before their transport, in two rooms, which Berta had arranged with such care and skill, as if they were planning to live there another twenty years. When Kristýna expressed her doubts whether it was worth it, Berta replied, But of course! Even if I were to live here only one more day. Kristýna took this to heart. It helped her hold on to the belief that her own life had some kind of value even during those moments when external circumstances suggested otherwise.

Berta's husband went to sleep in the adjoining room. Kristýna, as she always did when she slept over, pulled out an old straw mattress and made up a bed on the floor, while Berta stretched out on the red sofa. As soon as they turned out the light, Berta began to cry. She cried for the three full hours remaining. In order not to disturb Kristýna, she smothered her sobs in her pillow.

Kristýna listened, paralyzed. She had no idea what to do. She had never perceived any signs of weakness in Berta, and she wasn't sure Berta wanted her to see this one. And what could she possibly say? How could she console her? Could she even find the right words? Could any words compete with this absurdity, with the insanity of the war?

How is it possible, Kristýna says to herself, that I did not do that simplest thing, which any normal person would do right away, without thinking? Today, she would go and lie by her friend and embrace her. She would enfold and nurse her till the break of day and promise that everything would be all right, that nothing could happen to her. And she would say she loved her and would never leave her. She would give her a little of her strength for the terrible journey ahead. But at the time, she did nothing. She merely suffered in silence and anxiously watched the quickly paling wedge of the sky.

She had known Berta for exactly seven years. They had met shortly after Berta had moved from Vienna to Prague, when Kristýna was twenty and Berta thirty-four. She had seemed remarkably grown-up, and Kristýna had the feeling that she'd never be as mature as Berta. In Kristýna's eyes, Berta's life was already behind her. What a youth she'd had, thirty-four. The old Kristýna has to smile. Fourteen years later, when she was Berta's age, she felt much less mature than at twenty. Divorced, with a small child, she had the feeling she couldn't do anything, didn't know anything, and all of her previous experience was of no use. It was as if she were learning to walk again.

At one time, Berta had been absolutely everything to her: teacher, older sister, mother, a model she tried to compare herself to. But in the end, she knew her so little that she was not prepared to see her cry.

In later years, when Berta was no longer alive, Kristýna realized that she had always seen her friend as a half-mythical being. Her Berta she had met in 1934 in the studio of the painter K. But before that, another Berta existed. The one who grew up in the capital of the Austro-Hungarian Empire and came of age during the First World War, the one who used to visit Viennese cafés with her friends at a time when famous writers and artists frequented them, people who were either dead or also in exile by the 1930s.

Berta rarely spoke about her past. Maybe a little about the school in Weimar or Berlin in the mid-twenties, how she had met Brecht in the cafés there or the poet Else Lasker-Schüler, who called herself Prince Jussuf but looked like a frog. She talked about her experiences with the Communists, the 1934 uprising, and the days she had spent in police custody. She often came back to that. Everything else, Kristýna learned from her diaries.

Only several years after the war, when the pain of her loss was somewhat benumbed, Kristýna ventured to open the first of four red notebooks and began to reconstruct Berta's inner world retroactively, to connect the fragments she already knew. This world was not entirely comprehensible to her. Berta was only fourteen years older, but she had grown up in another era; she had moved in spheres that, despite all Kristýna's efforts, remained closed to her. Just as she could not imagine herself in Vienna in 1914, she could not really imagine the excitement over the first abstract painting, the airplane, or voting rights for women. To understand Berta and her contemporaries, she would have had to experience with them all those transformations, all those beginnings, and the euphoria that accompanied them. But in the 1930s, when Kristýna was coming of age, Europe was already darker, much more distressing, somewhere else.

CHAPTER 4

Berlin

MAX TOSSES AND GROANS FITFULLY beside her. She follows the tangled path of his sleep: caves, rough hillsides, steep cliffs, curtains of darkness he must pass through, beyond which lies something horrifying. She follows him, breath after breath. The image he is moving through is organic. It is not the dream of an artist of the new era—clear, composed, rectilinear. Dreams betray us, thinks Berta. We long for something new, but our dreams are woefully outdated. Both our dreams and our bodies.

Her body has the same longings as at the beginning of time.

She gets out of bed. It's not their mutual bed; it's her bed, in which Max sometimes sleeps when staying over.

She pulls back the curtain separating the imaginary bedroom from the rest of the room. Moonlight streams through the window in the ceiling, illuminating the white sheets of paper scattered about the two desks and the floor.

That's why I can't sleep, thinks Berta. The moon is peering in.

Berta pours herself a glass of water in the corner that serves as a kitchen and finds her cigarette case among the papers on Max's desk.

She climbs into the old wing-backed chair left behind by the former owner. It's her nighttime burrow. She pulls her bare legs up beneath her and drapes her nightshirt over them. Lately she's been spending a lot of nights like this, sitting in the dark, smoking and imagining pictures she'll never paint. Sometimes she goes so far as to get up and bring over her sketchbook and pencil. But as soon as she turns on the light and sees the empty paper in front of her, all her ideas and desire to record them vanish. And sometimes she cries for no reason at all. She hardly ever used to cry, but now it's as if something in her has started to melt away and she cries often. Mostly after lovemaking. As soon as her momentary spasm subsides, Berta sees things somehow oddly from the outside—herself, Max, and their intertwined bodies—and she starts to cry. Moaning, twitching, sometimes even choking. Nerves.

Her body has primeval longings.

In the dark armchair, Berta, in her white shirt, looks like an egg with smoke rising above it. She sees herself in the mirror on the opposite wall.

She is trying to deceive her body, but it takes its revenge. Berta knows this, and in desperation she wonders what to do. She sees only one way out, but that does not present itself. It even refuses itself to her.

Berta finishes smoking, extinguishes her cigarette, and clasps her arms around both knees, huddling up around the void that is her body. The emptiness that wants.

The old man has died. I write in the train on the way to his funeral. I write and try to summon up his face, his features, his voice. But the only thing I see is his venerable mustache. As if it were alive. And his left hand with his seal ring. I imagine the weight of his hand on my head. We used to go on walks every Sunday, always the same route, to Stephanplatz and back. He would lean on me as on a milestone while we walked. That was before he

*remarried. As for the years that followed, the feeling that
returns most often is the sense that I did not belong at
home, that I was superfluous. The loneliness, which he
made no easier for me.*

After everything that Berta lived through from the moment she
left home, she thinks about her father with much greater affec-
tion that she had previously been capable of. She no longer
sees him as merely a grouchy old man weighed down by worries, a man who was never very interested in her and who, she
believed, didn't like her very much among the other children.
She never ceased longing for the love she desired, but she had
to appreciate retrospectively how he believed in her. He was
genuinely convinced that her talent and diligence were enough
to make her an extraordinary woman. Only now she realizes
that her father never once indicated that she should marry and
start a family.

No more than three times during his life did they have a
serious conversation. The first was when she decided to give up
photography, the second when she informed him she was leaving for Germany, and the third during one of her last visits. This
conversation affected her so deeply that she can recall it word
for word. Suddenly, her father began to see her as an adult and
would pose questions to her. It was unpleasant, as if he were
demeaning himself in front of her on purpose. Did he, too, succumb to the postwar adoration of youth, which was henceforth
supposed to show the confused and delinquent elders the way?

He would ask her what was going to happen to Europe.
If Austria would join Germany and whether Italy could be
trusted. He wanted to know the definition of a nation. Who
was financing the fascists and how did the Communists imagine state administration? What did she think about Zionism?

He was not as narrow-minded as she'd thought. The venerable, royal mustache did not adorn an Austro-Hungarian relic, but a living, thinking head. The war awakened it to life, but what kind of life? When Otto Altmann understood his world was founded on assumptions that no longer applied, he did not take shelter in self-deception like so many of his peers, but, rather, demolished the whole construction with exemplary fair-mindedness. In childhood, he had converted to Catholicism with his parents, but he did not consider himself a believer. His faith was in the hopes with which the nineteenth century entered the twentieth: the emancipation of man and an integrated Europe. The war had ripped this faith from him, but he could not live without it; he was not mentally equipped for this and was searching for something to take its place. In the last years of his life, he returned to Judaism and persevered in it, even though he felt it was a lie. He went to the synagogue and prayed, but he did not feel any hope, just chaos and fear.

Berta observes the green banks of the Elbe. She realizes that it wouldn't take much for her and her father to understand each other. She thinks about Max, whom she left in Berlin, and the commission he now has to complete and turn in without her. She is the one who keeps track of deadlines; Max always has plenty of time for everything. But perhaps the theater will prod him along. Dress rehearsals are supposed to begin in a couple of days and everything still has to be made. Berta pulls out her sketchbook and pencil from her satchel. She scribbles on the edges of the paper, longing to lose herself in her work for at least a moment, but nothing comes to her. Her father is here. And Max. After a long time, she goes somewhere without him and keeps looking for him subconsciously; now and then she turns to say something to him. When they're together, they say aloud everything they're thinking. They casually toss words around, and at the same time each knows what the other is thinking. They laugh at references that strike others as nonsensical. They have their own language, their own system of references, their own history. Their own country, thinks Berta. Their own private country, the fruit of their mutual labor. In this country, they live like husband and wife. Max's other life, his marriage and three-year-old son, are out there. This does not belong to them. Even though it sometimes hurts.

Oh, it hurts. She's almost used to the excruciating pain. With time, it will certainly abate. Her pain is merely the remains of jealously, and jealousy is an antiquated, proprietorial instinct that does not suit her and that has no place in the workings of modern man, says Max. She agrees. She, too, wants to live freely, beyond all ossified and outworn formulas. Those ugly thoughts drag her down against her will. Especially when she's alone.

If marriage is such a retrograde institution, why did he marry in the first place?

From a sudden confusion of reason. People even commit suicide from such derangement. Why shouldn't he marry?

But why doesn't he want to get divorced now?

His wife would take his son from him.

Isn't that also just a proprietorial instinct?

Despite her best intentions, Berta cannot love Max's son, Joachim, whom they call Jo. He is perhaps the only child on Earth for whom she does not burn with excitement.

No, it's a fatherly love.

And is her love any less?

She cannot understand it because she has no children.

Perhaps she wanted a child.

He already has one. And doesn't want to lose it. Is she perhaps unhappy with him?

No, she's happy. But something is still missing.

Marriage?

Then get married; you had plenty of opportunities, Max yells at her. Put on an apron and get behind the stove. Hop into the marital bed. Put curlers in your hair, go dancing on Saturday, and roast him a goose on Sunday! Breed a horde of children beneath the duvet with him. Wipe their butts. But you can forget about art! In art, there is no room for housewives.

He's right, thinks Berta. If she has to decide between life with him and marriage the only way she can imagine it, she will always and again choose him.

I can't see what my divorce would do for you, Max says, trying to make up to her. Even if I got divorced, nothing would change between us. I can't spend more time with you, because I'm with you almost all the time as it is. I wouldn't become any more appealing to you—on the contrary. It would benefit neither our work nor our love. Otherwise, we could get married right away.

They both laugh. The idea of becoming Mrs. Jauner seems ridiculous even to Berta. She's already past that phase.

Three years in Berlin. It took a while before she got used to the city even a little. After Vienna, everything there seemed somehow crude and ugly, from the homemade dresses of the local ladies to the tasteless building facades. The streets were too wide, the wind bitter, and the coffee weak. For the first time, she had to admit that Vienna wasn't as awful as she'd always thought, and she missed its old elegance, its hedonistic character, which Berlin lacked entirely. Max was excited by Berlin. He claimed that only here, on the construction site of a new Europe, could genuine, original, and epochal ideas emerge, those that would stand up against all buffeting and foul weather. Not like that polite chin-wagging in Vienna. Ugliness is a better breeding ground for the spirit than beauty, claimed Max, because it liberates. In Vienna man is a slave to the past; he is afraid to lift a finger, out of deference to its astonishing creations.

One lives more impetuously in Berlin than in Vienna. People associate without constraint and prejudice; in Max's community, there are theater buffs, students, journalists, political agitators, dancers, photographers, writers, as well as the sons and daughters of bankers. What brings them together is a passion for art and politics. They are eccentric and nervous; cigarettes, coffee, alcohol, and now and then something stronger, substitute for food and sleep.

Berta and Max work in a studio Max had rented before her arrival. Berta even lives there, and Max comes regularly.

She has been to his home once at most. He took her there straight from the train station for supper and introduced her to his pregnant wife. After supper, the exhausted dancer went to lie down, and Max and Berta set out on a walk through the nighttime city. He took her to a café, then a bar; he introduced her to his friends. Only when the first birds began to chirrup and the sky above the city grew light did they climb the stairs to their first common abode, where that very morning they became lovers. Meinlich, the mutual promise of chastity, that was childhood, and now they could smile about it.

Were you surprised you were not the first? Were you convinced, despite everything you did to me, that I loved you and that you were irreplaceable? It hurt you, didn't it? That Berta did not remain faithful to your memory, that she did not become a widowed virginal nun. And I felt a moment of satisfaction. You did not want to ask, but I saw you were thinking about it. It pleased me how furious

you were. It was my revenge. I am aware of how pitiful it
is, but I will not allow it to be taken from me.

Otto Altmann did not arouse great passions when he was
alive, nor did he after death. The funeral came off without surprises. The will was concrete and specific, the property divided
precisely according to family hierarchy. Nobody was favored
and nobody forgotten. The amount of money left to Berta was
not great, but it was enough. If, for example, she decided to
return to Vienna and set something up there, Hugo Rosenthaal, the family notary, told Berta after he had unsealed and
read Altmann's will. She has called him uncle since childhood.

Young Austria needs its young people, especially people who
are educated, talented, and knowledgeable about what is going
on abroad. Filled with ideas and energy. They should build
something great right here and not elsewhere, he said.

Uncle Rosenthaal was a Social Democrat.

She promised to think about it.

At times, she actually did consider returning to Vienna, or,
rather, escaping from Berlin. She thinks about it during her
moments of courage, when she can imagine life without Max.

She also understood what Rosenthaal had in mind. For her,
too, a new Austria represented a concept of obligation beyond
personal desire or individual will. Unlike the ancient, mythi-
cally established monarchy, the new republic was fragile in its
incipience and exceedingly malleable. There was the constant
sense that one must sacrifice at least part of one's abilities for its
future, if not all of them.

She was also drawn toward Vienna by the hope, strength-
ened all the more by impatience, that if she freed herself from
her torment with Max, she might finally begin to paint.

Meeting at the Café Herrenhof

When Berta wanted to go with Maja to a café in 1917, they had to ask Rudi to accompany them. Despite their short hair and skirts, they never would have ventured in alone. To go to a café alone before the end of the war would still have suggested they were looking to meet someone.

Ten years later Berta sits alone at the Café Herrenhof, and it suggests nothing more than that she came here to drink coffee and read the newspapers. She can even light up a cigarette and still be a lady, if the term *lady* has not become somewhat corroded over the last decade.

She is just about to get up to return the *Revue des Deux Mondes* to the newspaper table when she notices someone peculiar. He is standing in the middle of the café, amid the marble tables, and looking around, casting his eyes about, apparently looking for someone to sit down with. He looks eccentric, like someone who has just come back from the Soviet Union, thinks Berta. Every now and then in Berlin, one of her or Max's acquaintances would emerge wearing a Russian fur cap, a *rubashka* shirt, and tattered felt boots. They had left in suits with full suitcases and then returned dressed in all sorts of ways. They had given away everything they'd brought with them to their Soviet comrades, their new brothers and sisters, who hadn't seen the conveniences of modern civilization for several years.

Truth be told, it is not possible to overlook the man standing among the marble tables of the Café Herrenhof. On this warm May morning, he is dressed in a long military overcoat, leather boots, a *rubashka* shirt, and a red scarf around his neck. Topping it all off is a flat-billed cap of the type worn by Lenin. Gray stubble adorns his pale, sunken cheeks. Powerful nervous excitement can be felt in the way he holds his body, in the sharp jerks of his head when he looks around the room, in his entire figure and, primarily, in his eyes, blazing behind round glasses.

Berta rises, and the movement draws the man's attention. He looks at her as if trying to recall how he knows her, and to Berta, he seems familiar. Actually only the eyes. Isn't it—no, that's impossible. He couldn't have changed so much!

Then he recognizes her.

His face lights up with an intense, childlike joy, and he quickly makes his way over to her, as if he is throwing aside the tables and chairs that stand in his way.

Berta Altmann! My best student!

Berta blushes.

Robert Meinlich! Theodor Noor!

He sits down across from her and orders black coffee and a glass of water.

He is beaming. Berta Altmann! One of the few people I'm always glad to see. Goodness! What are you doing here? Have you returned from Berlin? And what about Jauner? Do you still see him now and then? You two were inseparable, after all, until he got married, yes? Strange! I never would have expected it from him. That wife of his, I remember her well! A bourgeois bimbo. So tell me what's been going on!

Berta tells him about herself and about Max, how they're working together and somehow living together, too.

Meinlich listens attentively.

Why doesn't he get a divorce? he asks.

He has a son.

Meinlich barely suppresses a grin. Who doesn't have one son or another somewhere? As if that matters. Children and their parents should be kept apart. Parents corrupt their children and children corrupt their parents. There are specialists for child rearing. But Jauner will forever be a mere member of the petite bourgeoisie. He gets that from his family. Are you painting?

We're designing costumes, scenery, interiors, and so on. Max does the larger pieces, and I work out the details.

You wait on him?

I work with him.

That's the same thing. You should teach, says Meinlich, leaning back in his chair and fixing his eyes on her, as if to lend his words the greatest weight. You always had that type of enthusiasm that can be conveyed to others. And you are neither envious nor selfish. Just like I am, even though no one wants to believe me. You're not ordinary. You understand that one must sacrifice oneself for greater things, for humanity, and personal feelings must be placed aside. We live in a great time. Everything we longed for is within reach. The kingdom of light, as I once taught you. In only one thing was I mistaken: The path to good does not lead through asceticism and prayer. It is bloody. It is a path of violence and great sacrifice.

Meinlich declaims in a raised voice, so that everyone can hear him: We could have won already if it were not for that liar Bauer and his band of cowards who call themselves Social Democrats. Ugh!

This surprises Berta. Until now, she always thought the Social Democrats—the second-largest party in the country and the ruling party in Vienna—were proceeding perhaps carefully, but essentially in the right direction. Under their rule, Vienna has become a genuine town of workers, evidence that it is possible to tax champagne, casinos, and horse races to construct apartments, hospitals, libraries, and schools.

You must understand, violence is necessary, Meinlich says, inclining his head toward her, as if reading her thoughts. I don't like it myself. I've never eaten meat, and I could never hurt a fly. But I've gradually come to realize that revolution without violence is impossible. And the establishment of the dictatorship of the proletariat is impossible without revolution. Bauer jabbers on about parliament, but the parliament is nonsense. Unless the parliament abolished itself. The difference between us and the Social Democrats is that we want to abolish capitalism, whereas Bauer does everything to preserve it. Bauer lies to the workers. Bauer does everything only for appearances, to deceive the workers. And the rich assist him because they know well enough that as long as the people believe Bauer, they will not join us. And they will not take up weapons.

Therefore, we cannot budge! We let slip away the best moment, immediately after the war, when the bourgeoisie was on its knees and the entire country was demanding change. It was then we should have taken power! And who prevented it? Otto Bauer. Otto Bauer, bribed by factory owners and quarry magnates who lied to the workers and said that the time was not yet ripe, that they had no hope for victory, and that it would be better to come to an agreement with the capitalists. Since then, they bribe the workers, offer them crumbs of that which they should have seized themselves long ago, and have postponed the revolution indefinitely. This is Marxism the Austrian way. The wolf eats its fill and leaves the goat untouched. The workers, says Bauer, will rise up only if the fascists take power in Austria. We will resort to violence, says Bauer straightforwardly, if our state—with its party system, parliament, and laws—is threatened. The laws, which have a single goal: to protect the interests of the bourgeoisie. But we will never resort to violence, says Bauer, to abolish this rotten state and establish a new, just state, a state of the workers and farmers. Bauer has still not openly acknowledged whose side he is on or how stupid he is! He wants the capitalists to defend themselves against the fascists, against their own. Didn't the capitalists invent fascism for their own protection? Is he just naive, or is he being disingenuous? The only danger he mentions is a fascist putsch. But fascists learn quickly. What that idiot Hitler tried in Munich in '23 will not be repeated. They'll wait for the right moment. The center of power will move imperceptibly, bit by bit, so as not to frighten the public. Local scuffles will break out here and there; the militia will beat someone up; a law will be passed that will change nothing by itself but, instead, with other similar laws, will weave a firm web that will someday entrap us all. Bauer first of all. You cannot reason with evil!

The main thing is that blood not flow, they say. There's already been enough blood! No, there hasn't. More and more will flow. What is fascism? Money. And money will be defended to the last drop of blood. If they have to murder half of Europe, they will do it. Here it is no longer a matter of the individual, of individual rich people, but of money itself. The psychology of money, its logic, which sets the entire machinery of violence in motion. Money will never surrender. Money always wants more and more money. To money, a human life means nothing, not even millions of lives. It unleashed the first war and it will unleash the second and the third. If necessary. And each of these wars will be bloodier than the last. Nothing will stop it, not laws, not faith, nothing. Only one thing can stop money: its liquidation. The system that provides it with such power must be abolished. Eradicate evil once and for all. Violence can be stopped only with violence. The battle against capitalism is a battle against money. It is a battle for everything! For every future life.

Meinlich looks exhausted. He rests his forehead on his palm and sits a moment, unmoving. He still has the power to persuade, and Berta has no doubt that what he says is true. The debates of her friends in Berlin proceed along the same lines, and she still hasn't become a member of the Communist Party herself, only because she doesn't know of what use she could be to the Communists.

Meinlich finishes his water.

Blood is flowing and Bauer does nothing. In Schattendorf, at the last workers' protest in February, the fascists beat a helpless old man and child. They caught the thugs and now they're standing before the court. But I will be surprised if they're not released. That's really how things stand in this country. Vienna is not all of Austria, Berta! But if these thugs are released, Bauer will no longer be able to lie his way out of it. It will be proof of how far things have gone! I have to go now. But come have a look at one of our meetings. Perhaps tomorrow at seven in the evening. You'll see what we're doing, what our agenda is. You could come work for us. We need reliable people.

He pulls a pencil from his pocket and scribbles an address on the check.

You must come. And if Jauner wants to come, bring him along. He's a bougie, but right now we can use everyone we can find.

Max is in Berlin.

True.

Meinlich says good-bye, shakes her hand, and kisses her in the Soviet manner, once on each cheek.

Come join us, Berta. You're really going to like it. This isn't any Berlin bohemianism, but the genuine people. You'll see how deeply they can move you. It will be good for you and your art. There you can genuinely be useful.

She promises she will attend the meeting. She will be here until the end of the week; then she's going back to Berlin.

You should return to Vienna, Berta, says Meinlich on the

way out. I mean because of Jauner, too. This won't lead anywhere. You must find a husband and start a family. Ignore his
protests. You can deceive a woman, but not nature.

Meinlich taps her on the shoulder, exits through the revolv-
ing door, and steps into the street.

His red bandanna distinguishes him from everyone in the
crowd until he rounds the corner.

CHAPTER 5

The Accident

SHE WAS NUTS, Grandma, says Milena.

She sits in Kristýna's chair, reading Berta's diaries. And conjuring up Aaron.

Kristýna knows her granddaughter means no harm, but she still feels like hitting her.

Stop reading it, she says.

But it's interesting.

I shouldn't have lent it to you. You can't understand it yet.

And you can? asks Milena. Why a woman would spend so many years with a married man who didn't want to live with her. Because of him, she had one abortion after another, so in the end she couldn't have any children at all. That seems normal to you?

She didn't know that. Back then, they didn't know much about those things, says Kristýna.

Then explain it to me, says Milena, challenging her. You knew her. She must have had some serious issues with herself. Maybe she thought she was really ugly and couldn't find anybody else except Jauner.

Did Berta find herself ugly? She wasn't exactly pretty, but she wasn't ugly, either. She was so animated and kindhearted that everyone must have seen her as an attractive woman. She had beautiful eyes. She never spoke about her appearance, but perhaps it played a role in her life. Sometimes she made fun of how small she was and her short legs. But they would just laugh about it. Kristýna was simply unable to see her friend as an ordinary woman. She had too high an opinion of her to suspect that vanity played any part. But maybe it had, and if Jauner fostered that impression in her . . .

Kristýna has known several women who stayed with their husbands only because they managed to make them feel they were ugly and undesirable. Men's self-confidence has had a hundred-year head start on women's, thinks Kristýna. Even the biggest idiot and gargoyle among men can always find a woman who will make him feel he's a god. And even the best among women will always find a man who can destroy her with only a few words. But Berta and Jauner's relationship couldn't be explained that way. That would be too simple.

I don't think you can understand, she finally replies, if you don't consider the times in which Berta grew up and lived. It was not a conservative time—quite the opposite, in fact. People slept and lived together out of wedlock. In the community in which Berta and Jauner moved, it was perfectly normal. Everything was starting over again; it was one big experiment. Traditional marriage had been written off, but no other alternative had yet been developed. They tried everything, everything that a relationship could sustain, and children were somewhat superfluous. Nobody knew what to do with them. Liberation for women also meant liberation from childbearing. Mainly that. Women like Berta understood it acutely and clearly: either a family or work and freedom.

So it wasn't just the scumbag's decision.

I don't know how it was. Berta and I never talked about it,

and she didn't say very much about it in her diaries. A lot of things you simply have to assume.

You think she didn't want children, as well?

At first, she definitely didn't. And if she could have decided freely—that is, if it were even possible to decide such things freely—she probably wouldn't have wanted children even later on. It was despite herself that she began longing for a child. And the more complicated and impossible it became, the more she wanted it. Until it became an obsession.

I see, but still . . . Milena shakes her head. Going out with a married man for so long isn't normal.

She wasn't going out with him, explains Kristýna. She was working with him.

And sleeping with him.

Well, yes.

It's the same thing, says Milena, terminating the debate. In any case, she was pathologically dependent on him.

Don't you think that love might look like that? asks Kristýna.

Like that? scoffs Milena, meaning: impossible, miserable, hopeless from the very start? She becomes absorbed in her thoughts.

What can you possibly know? Kristýna says to herself. You're as stupid as I was when I presumed to tell Berta she was unhappy. I had my own idea of happiness, which did not at all resemble Berta's caring but somewhat indifferent cohabitation. After all, she herself complained she wasn't satisfied. She achieved nothing that she'd wanted—she became neither a great artist nor a mother. She doubted herself. The main thing, she confided in me, is that I not give up children for anyone or anything. You must have children, she said, believe me. You might not see the importance of it now, but later you'll start to feel lost. You can go wherever you want; nothing really matters, nothing is tying you down, but you hate your freedom. Everything dissolves in it, even the zest for life.

Kristýna gave birth to and raised a son, but she's not sure life without him would have been so bad. She often longed for the freedom that Berta cursed. After she gave birth, her life became a constant battle. She was certain she would have given her life for Mirek without thinking twice, but she could not sacrifice her work for him. He threatened what she loved, what she lived for. Only when Milena was born did she realize she hadn't enjoyed and reveled in her son's childhood at all. She was always tense when her son did not allow her to paint; she was lost to herself, if only in her imagination, and didn't pay proper attention to what he was doing, how he was developing and growing up. It was different with her granddaughter. She was fascinated by the being taking shape before her; she found it as fascinating and enriching as her own art. When her daughter-in-law went back to work, Kristyna devoted herself to little Milena body and soul, joyously, and without a second thought. Her own son, she noticed only intermittently. Joyfully and guiltily at the same time. She saw him as a debt she would never be able to repay.

The summer passes, and Milena has no news about Aaron. She hasn't written to him, either. She has his e-mail address, but she doesn't know where to renew their interrupted conversation. The longer she waits, the more difficult it seems. The words she would be capable of writing seem too formal, abstract, too distant from those she uses when she addresses him in her mind. When composing her unsent e-mails, it's as if she has gone back several luminous years, when Aaron is not the Aaron she made love with. He is almost a stranger. She has no idea how important their mutual experience was; it's all so indistinct. They hadn't had time to establish a common language, discrete roles. It is beyond her to decide the way in which their relationship should develop further. She is waiting for a sign from him, but he is silent.

He's gone back to his girlfriend and is trying to put me out of his mind, she says to herself, as if out of obligation. This explanation suggests itself, but she can't believe it: Didn't he say he belonged to her? Words she'd attributed no significance to when they were uttered are becoming a pledge. At the same time, she cannot say she loves Aaron, and she pretends even to herself that nothing actually happened.

At the end of September, a package containing a videocassette and a large postcard of nighttime Tel Aviv finds its way to Kristýna's address. Viki writes that they managed to sell the film to several television stations, and she and Noah are satisfied with the result. If not for Kristýna's and Milena's help, they wouldn't have been able to film half of it. Milena attributes the fact that Viki mentioned Aaron for no apparent reason to a display of intelligence usually referred to as "women's": The cameraman is still traveling; he had quite a full summer. America, then Mexico, and now he's in Germany. Since they finished filming in the Czech Republic, they haven't seen him once. It's good he has work, especially now, with the crisis everywhere, but maybe he's taking on too much. Money and work aren't everything, and he's well on his way to exhaustion.

So he's still on the road and not at home with his girlfriend. The weeks have probably flown by and he doesn't realize how long it's been since he's seen her.

Kristýna's injury has nothing to do with the package. She watched the film with Milena Saturday morning and in the afternoon set out on a walk to the Tiché Valley. She needed to determine the shape of a certain cliff there. It was to the left above a pond. She could recall fairly precisely the color (bluish, with golden clumps of grass) and especially the structure of the face; she just wasn't positive about the shape. It was Kristýna's autumn cliff. She used to lie on it in the fall and watch the green fade from the surrounding forest as it was consumed by ocher, crimson, lemon yellow, and dark purplish brown. The sky would be a spidery, clear blue, and the warmth from the heated cliff would flow into her body. Kristýna loves stones; they always seem to her filled with a special force. Milena offered to accompany her, but Kristýna refused. She wanted to be alone. It had nothing to do with the film.

It's true she was upset in the morning. She didn't like the film *Berta Altmann: Artist and Teacher*. One could almost say it wounded her.

She had finally justified her unfortunate performance before the camera to herself by the thought that the film would perhaps at least bring attention to Berta's paintings and contribute to her posthumous fame. But this justification fell away when she saw the completed film.

She hadn't expected Noah and Viki, as she remembered them, to create a masterpiece, but she was not prepared for the simplification and manipulation they had committed. Her own appearance had been edited down to what she'd said about Berta's personal life. Exactly what she shouldn't have talked about.

Of all the interpretations offered, the Israelis had chosen the most banal: They had made Berta out to be a victim from beginning to end. First a heartless father and stepmother, then self-absorbed teachers, the egotistical Jauner, the calculating Communists, and finally the Nazis. A pitiful being who fought mostly with her own deep-seated uncertainty, which kept her from realizing herself as a woman or as a painter. Someone who had to try to solve her problems with the help of psychoanalysis (Kristýna had divulged even this!). They had reduced Berta's lifelong struggle, which in Kristýna's eyes was not without elements of magnificence, to something petty, personal, soiled.

These people know absolutely nothing and then decide to make a film about Berta! Berta Altmann, whose complicated personality not even Kristýna could fathom completely. Who loved her. Those blockheads, those film people, those traffickers in the fates of others think it's enough to fly to the Czech Republic for two weeks and then spend another week in Vienna.

Even on the visual side, the movie seemed a hodgepodge. Window reflections, puddles quivering and dissolving, breaking up and finally alternating with Berta's paintings: train stations, trees, configurations of roofs. If it's supposed to mean something, she'd certainly like to know what. And airborne clouds and railroad tracks, tracks heading here and there, even a broken chain fluttering in the wind. Kitsch, splutters Kristýna. Edited like a TV commercial, with not a single shot lasting more than two seconds.

Milena quite liked the documentary; it was nothing revolutionary, but it was enjoyable. Why not? You can do what you want. You don't have to take everything so seriously, she told Kristýna.

Then why do they do it if they don't take it seriously? complained Kristýna. And why did they choose Berta to suffer for it?

Kristýna had actually gotten quite upset this morning. But after lunch, she seemed calm, and when she set off around three o'clock to Vítězné Square to catch the bus to Roztoky, she felt quite all right.

Fortunately, the bus was moving rather slowly; in fact, it was almost standing still. Nevertheless, it knocked her down on the sidewalk. She fell hard and felt a pain in her hip. She couldn't get up. Some bystanders called an ambulance. They took her to the hospital in Střešovice, because it was the closest, and got it x-rayed.

Nothing serious, said the young doctor as they were signing her in. We'll give you an artificial joint. You'll have to do some rehabilitation; then you'll be able to run for another ten years. Goodness, a broken hip joint is the most trivial injury that can happen to an elderly woman. On the other hand, you wouldn't believe how often people die from it.

She sits in his white-and-yellow kitchen, framed by the doors to the balcony. Against the crisp blue sky is the silhouette of a woman; he sees the tall, slender woman wrapped in his bathrobe, which she slips from her brown shoulders, the outline of a woman with short black hair and an expressive face sitting in the yellow light of the morning sun in his kitchen; yellow, white, black, and blue; a narrow face with perfect eyebrows, pointed shoulders and teeth; a white cup with black coffee; embittered wrinkles around the mouth. The doors to the balcony are open. An unfamiliar woman sits in the doorway.

Aaron!

The first woman with whom he felt safe after his wife had unexpectedly left him and taken their son. A reliable girlfriend who understands his passion for his work completely and even shares it. An elegant, mature woman. He sought safety in her maturity. In her self-sufficiency and self-confidence was a guarantee of a happy life.

Lu?

By the time she was thirty-five, she had reached precisely the position in her profession that would allow her to start a family and at the same time stay on top. Even her relationship with Aaron was developing in a satisfactory manner. Everything was arranged, everything functioned, they both had jobs they loved, and they respected each other. Up to now, he had managed to arouse her in bed, so much so that she never even considered looking at other men, and that was something for her. She was happy. But she wanted more. She wanted to buy a large apartment with Aaron, with high ceilings, where she could also work on her photos, so she wouldn't always have to leave home for work. She wanted a housekeeper who would show up every day, someone reliable. And she wanted a child. Right now. She was dying to press the warm, soft body against her own.

Aaron!

Lu?

I just want to say . . . nothing. It will pass.

Do you think so?

I'm positive.

I don't deserve you!

When they start talking about how they don't deserve you, they're just looking for an excuse to leave you, thinks Lu. And she decides to pretend it's nothing. She will not change her plans, plans she's worked on for so many years, because of Aaron's momentary breakdown. If he really had met someone else, it was definitely during one of his trips, which means the woman is safely far away, in Mexico or America or wherever he's been flying about for the past six months. She saw him only briefly during his trips. Once she was menstruating, so they didn't even try to sleep together, and she didn't notice anything special the second time. It wasn't the greatest sex of her life, but after such a long time together, what else could you expect? Only now that Aaron's back and not planning a trip anytime soon, it turns out there's a problem. He can't make love to her. It simply doesn't work. Without mincing words: Aaron is impotent. It's surprising, shocking when she remembers what she's gone through with him. He fondles her, tries to satisfy her in other ways, but Lu doesn't care for it. Now it's not so much a matter of pleasure as of a child. And he's not going to give her one with his finger.

Lu?

When it happened the first and second time, she didn't get the least upset. She'd read that such disorders are normal for men after forty. Only a few weeks later did she start to worry and tried to get him to see a doctor. But Aaron said it was no good, there was no point. And this aroused her suspicions. Any normal guy would start freaking out, but not him. He was calm, sad, resigned somehow. As if he didn't care if he would ever sleep with her again. Lu controls herself, but inside she tortures Aaron to death in a thousand different ways. She hates him. But she copes with it. She's not going to destroy everything, leave him, meet someone else, break up, get together, and readjust. There's no time for that!

Once she even asked him if the problem was with her. He swore it wasn't. She was perfect, still as attractive as the first time they met. It's just something in his body or soul, something he can't put his finger on and which is not up to him. It's not under his control.

Lu takes pride in the fact that everything in her life is under control, everything. Consequently, there must be a way out of this situation.

Lu?

I think you should go to the doctor, dear.

Lu, listen to me. Maybe it's nothing. Maybe I'm making the whole thing up. But you deserve to know.

Why can't he sort this out himself? Why does he have to bother her with it?

I think I fell in love.

Here it comes. The confession she's heard so many times before: from her own men, from the men of others, from men on television. Perhaps there will be tears. Does Lu need this? She does. Because she has decided to hold on. To start a family. She summons up the image of a baby's warm body. A being that belongs to her unconditionally.

Most of all, she'd like to collect her things and leave.

And that's it. Aaron smiles.

This is what she dreads the most. The inability of men to articulate their own feelings and facilitate an active approach. They don't know what's going on with themselves until it's too late. Instead of saying I met a girl, I liked her, I wanted to do it and I did, and it was great, he remains silent. And this silence turns an ordinary sexual transgression into something mysterious, which is going to take over his life.

Lu knows it is impossible to do battle with an unknown enemy. The enemy must first be discovered, even if it might tear her heart out: Who is it? she asks him. Where is she from?

Prague.

A Jew?

No.

Are you still in contact?

No.

No?

I haven't heard from her since I left Prague. It's already been six months.

She hasn't contacted you?

No.

What did you two have together?

I made love to her once.

Once?

Yes.

Did you promise each other anything?

No. We didn't discuss the future at all; it was odd.

Lu is not interested in how Aaron's experience was odd: Do you think your—she wants to say impotence, but it seems too cruel—that your inability is somehow connected to this?

It's possible.

That would be really strange, wouldn't it?

It's possible.

Dead silence. Then the outline of the woman against the light blue background slowly rises, walks over to the seated Aaron, and presses her firm, flat belly against his right ear. In imitation of a maternal gesture, she encircles his head with her slender, cold fingers.

Do you want to know what I think, dear? I think you're terribly overworked, we haven't seen each other in a long time, and we've drifted apart somewhat. And that—don't be angry—you're having some sort of midlife crisis. I completely understand that this isn't pleasant for you, but that doctor Alicia recommended is good and very reliable. He gets excellent results. Josh has seen him, too.

Okay, Lu. The woman is a stranger, but he still doesn't want to hurt her. He doesn't want to hurt anybody.

Ever since getting back to Jerusalem, he's had a strange feeling of unreality. He'd like to lie down and dream, in silence, in peace.

Right after Lu leaves, when that woman goes home.

She accepts all the humiliation concerning her body as punishment.

The wound is healing badly; she has a fever and can't sleep. A rehabilitation nurse comes to see her twice a day and forces her to exercise through unbearable pain.

She threw out the hospital priest who came to comfort her. She had never liked Catholics. But he appeared again at night, together with a crowd of people, familiar and unfamiliar, who came to see her night after night. The dead and the living. Her parents, old friends, classmates from elementary and high school, as well as those from the Academy of Applied Arts, her teachers, her landlady, the postman who used to bring her mail forty years ago, when she was living with Mirek in Vinohrady. Her son visited her several times, at different ages. Once, she even experienced the poignant delight of breast-feeding, a feeling of disintegration. Somewhere in the background, her husband flitted about. Several of her lovers visited her, along with the curator of a South Moravian gallery and the porter from the factory where she'd worked in the fifties. Mirka's homeroom teacher. It was a remarkable medley, including faces from television, painted masks from Mexican television serials, weeping victims of wars and catastrophes, the mutually interchangeable faces of politicians.

Berta appeared to her twice. Once, her back was turned, but Kristýna was certain it was her. A dry, warm snow was falling, shredded wings. A vein-strewn sky. She wanted to detain her friend. She tried to call out to her, but she had no voice. Berta was walking away, tiny, lost on a winter path. Then she disappeared and left Kristýna all alone. Unforgiven.

The second time, she saw her from afar. She was running in a group of people stripped naked, their hands above their heads. They disappeared into the open gates of a low, oblong building. Flames flickered and a black smoke was rising from a nearby chimney.

When the priest came a third time, she asked him what he could offer her.

Relief, he said.

And how can you arrange that? Can you turn back time?

God's mercy is unfathomable, he replied.

He had a badly shaven and nicked face. Sickly skin. Such skin must be a curse for a young person, Kristýna thought, feeling sorry for him. After all, sometime long ago, in the dusky antiquity of her childhood, her parents had had her baptized. They'd wrapped her in lace and ribbons and sprinkled her with holy water—she had the photograph at home as proof. She was a limb of the Church's body whether she liked it or not. And as such, she felt a certain obligation to listen to this young priest.

CHAPTER 6

Vienna

Berta moved back to Vienna in the fall of 1927 and with her inheritance established her own design studio: Berta Altmann—Tapestries, Textiles, Interior Design. She placed ads in the newspaper, began meeting with old acquaintances, and slowly built up a clientele that would ensure a steady supply of customers. She would meet with Meinlich and his Communist cell, sometimes go to their meetings at the Workers' House, and agreed once a week, on Saturday afternoons, to lead graphic art lessons for children of blue-collar workers. She was quite satisfied with this decision. The class preparation obliged her to think back to her own experiences and create some sort of method. She taught for free, on her own time, and no one could tell her what to do. Meinlich left everything up to her; he had entirely renounced his own artistic and pedagogical activities. He had ceased to believe that art could save humanity, and everything that did not lead directly to this objective was a waste of time.

The invitation came in the mail.

The card of expensive handmade paper was inscribed in a sweeping hand: Recently I acquired a statue of yours, Saint Anne, from the estate of an acquaintance, a Viennese art collector. The more I come to know the work, the more I long to make the acquaintance of the artist. I would be exceptionally delighted if you were to stop by for a visit! I receive visitors every Thursday from four to seven at Elizabethstrasse 22, fourth floor.

Berta sniffed the card; it gave off a faint aroma. Not unpleasant.

The mention of the statue was odd. For her, Saint Anne remained fixed in her consciousness like a boundary marker separating the period before Jauner's betrayal and after it. Berta had already grown used to its presence; it was a symbol. The actual form of the statue, she could recall only with difficulty.

She was flattered that the famous Viennese lady wanted to meet her, even though Berta and her friends looked down on the society to which she belonged. People who gathered at the salon of the Immortal One were "old"; their internal makeup did not correspond to the new era. After the collapse of the Austro-Hungarian Empire they felt homeless, nostalgic, for-ever tuned to a minor key. And all the more seriously did they occupy themselves with trivialities.

The perverse bourgeoisie, Meinlich used to say.

Berta belonged to the young.

Nevertheless, the redolent card had arrived from a vanished paradise where even she had her share of memories. And to be honest, those memories were dearer to her than all the meet-ings, all the engaged art and social justice put together.

The Meyers' voluptuously furnished home. Irena at the piano, music by Chopin and Mahler, days in which there was nothing but art, art that was sacred. Beauty was sacred. Beauty that was inaccessible, unique and unequaled, lofty and edifying, exclusive, unjust to the core.

She continued her reflections: the summer in Semmering.

How had they imagined their future back then? As art and

love. But they'd understood both as merely a game dangerous to life: To give everything for the sake of love and to die are the same thing. To live always on the edge, not like their sedentary mothers and fathers, in an empire where nothing had changed for centuries. To live life beyond measure. They'd craved untamed rhythms, movement!

She recalled the afternoon in the Café Central when Maja had referred to the most esteemed woman in Vienna as a sugar loaf. It was already dark when they went outside. Rudi insisted they walk Berta home, so they linked arms on either side of her. They were taller than she was, but they stayed in step, proceeding briskly and lightly. Their collaborative locomotion elated them. Nothing and nobody could stand in their way. At one point, Rudi took her hand and didn't let go until they reached the gates of her house.

She rings at the luxurious apartment on Elizabethstrasse on Thursday at five in the afternoon.

She has decided to stay for only a very brief time: thank her for the invitation, perhaps make some contacts that will come in handy later. The richest people in Vienna meet here; it wouldn't be a bad idea to acquire a couple of customers. Except that the taste of these people is frightfully limited. They live in old-fashioned, gaudy apartments filled with gilt-framed pictures, mirrors, chairs, and sideboards that look like coffins. They've got mounds of bric-a-brac collecting dust, where proper sunlight never penetrates, not even a waft of fresh air. Their apartments are as full of junk as their heads, and they have no concept of modern space or modern life, thinks Berta.

The only thing that makes the salon of the Immortal One different from other similar salons is that, alongside kitschy paintings by Hans Makart and the Viennese Secessionists, she has a few early works by the painter K. No abstracts. In the corner stands a bust of her departed husband by August Rodin and a female hand from the same workshop. Berta doesn't see her Anne anywhere. Most likely, it's been tidied away in some less significant spot, along with the works of other inconsequential artists who one day may become famous (in which case they will advance to the drawing room or the salon), or fame will elude them (the guest rooms, a dark corner of the foyer, then the definitive descent into the basement or up into the attic).

The Immortal One has gained much weight since the last time Berta saw her, ten years ago. She receives Berta alone in a richly embroidered house gown, some sort of royal cloak that merges with her powerful breast and covers what can be covered.

But above the unformed mass, atop her neck, which no longer resembles a smooth alabaster column, looms her head, which, despite the flaccid, almost blurry features, is imposing and magnificent, not beautiful in the ordinary sense of the word, but brave, proud, resembling the heads of Greek statues. Her lips are tiny, sharply delineated; the upper forms a perfect arc, called a Cupid's bow. Between the lower lip and the spherical, pronounced chin is a small dimple, which men swooned over in her time. Her nose is slightly askew, not small. Her high cheekbones are almost invisible below a layer of fat, but her eyes are beautiful, dark gray, clear, and gleaming, framed by thick, dark lashes. She's not made up, or if she is, you can't tell.

She gives Berta both hands.

I'm so glad you came and that no one's here right now. This is wonderful; we'll have a moment to ourselves. But come. First of all, I'll show you where I put your statue. Your remarkable statue, says the woman. She lowers her voice and closes her eyes, obviously meaning to intimate admiration. Your Saint

Anne fascinated me, she says, and leads Berta down a long hallway with rows of white, high, golden-handled and glass-paned doors bearing images of naked nymphs.

I must admit that at first it didn't even occur to me that this could be the work of a young woman, nearly a girl. Why, you were a student just five years ago. I thought it was the work of an old man, something in which he had invested all of his life experiences, his torment and loneliness. And it turns out to be you! You must have experienced something exceedingly painful to create a work so genuinely, so . . . poignantly alive. Oh, forgive me, I didn't mean to offend you. I'm just trying to tell you how close this statue is to my heart. It's an image of my own soul. And it knows what suffering is.

She opens one of the doors and they are standing in a room suffused with the rosy afternoon sun—her bedroom.

In the Bedroom of the Immortal One

Saint Anne, it is just a face and hands. The narrow ridges of her hands, fingers firmly together, straining, pointing upward, as if burning with a somber, placid flame. The hands border the woman's face on either side. And as they point to the sky, her face peers outward, toward the viewer, taut and charged, her closed eyes seem likely to explode, her firmly closed lips resisting the flow, the avalanche of words.

It is a face of pain, but exaggerated, ecstatic, placing itself at the center, elevating and dramatizing itself, thinks Berta.

She sees that the Saint Anne is outdated and overdone, too much influenced by Expressionism.

She feels how old she has grown over these last five years.

How could the Immortal One think an old man carved this expression of despair? Doesn't she see this is a depiction of pain that is still young? With no way out, without bitterness, without weariness, pure and keen as a lash.

We can stay here, suggests the Immortal One, and rings a bell. She orders the chambermaid to bring coffee and refreshments to the bedroom and to turn away other guests with the excuse that she is unwell.

Let them come another time.

The woman stares pensively past Berta's head, looking out the window. She speaks fluently, as if she had prepared her entire speech.

We women must help one another out. It's so difficult— our lot, I mean. How do you come to terms with it? That's what I'd like to know. That's why I wanted to talk to you. I've been thinking a lot lately, and my deliberations usually end with a single question. Please tell me, why did the Christians crucify a man? The symbol of human suffering is a man, but it is actually the woman who hangs on the cross. Bleeding, lacerated by childbirth, stripped of everything, exhausted, abandoned by her husband and children. That is the image of the worst thing nature or God can perpetrate on us. That is punishment. The cross. And it is the woman who carries it, not the man. But why? Why are we punished like this? What are we guilty of? If you ask any man, he'll start in with the serpent and the apple in paradise.

How have I sinned? I listened to my heart, nothing but my heart. Was my heart the serpent? Was it a sin to listen to it? If it was, I've paid for it a hundred times over. I yielded to love and thwarted all my abilities. My teachers said I had great talent. Before I met my first husband, I was obsessed with my work; I lived only for art, for it alone.

Now they say I'm obsessed with ingenious men. That I'm vain and adorn myself with borrowed plumes. But that's not

the way it is. I had to place everything in my life that mattered at the feet of my first husband. I fought and struggled,
but he won. As an artist, he knew what art demands from a
person, and he didn't want to share me. He was convinced that
he needed my entire, undivided being to be able to create. He
had no doubt that his work took precedence over mine. When
he died, the path back was closed. What was left for me? When
you cannot incarnate your own work, you use the work of others. You direct all your sensibilities, your intellect, your imagination, your exhilaration, all of your love toward the work that
should be yours but isn't. Or toward yourself.

When is a woman irresistible? What do you think? Not when
she loves, when she gives herself and sacrifices everything. No.
A woman is most attractive when she thinks only about herself,
when she's self-absorbed, when she applies all her energy, all her
creative power to her own persona. Then she seduces, inspires,
fascinates. After my first husband died, I had that power. Until
I met my poet.

Now I live only for him. I'm growing old, fading away, but
that's not important. I'm where I should be. I am fuel for the
fireplace of genius, the closest to happiness I've ever been. Don't
think I'm flattering myself that I could have been someone. I
don't regret sacrificing my powers for my husbands, who were
indeed superior to me. I've forgiven myself long ago. But there is
some kind of power, perhaps fate, that will not forgive me. Why
would they all have perished otherwise? I had so many children,
and they're all dead. Everything inside of me has burned out
so many times, and so many times have I risen from the ashes.
But never whole. My heart has always been somewhat colder,
more embittered, closer to death. Why my beautiful, innocent
children? Why not me?

Perhaps I was indeed created for art instead of love and

motherhood. Perhaps I should not have stepped aside when the first encumbrance ensnared my heart. And my body. My longing for pleasure is intense. It's difficult for me to overcome it even when it is procured with such torment. And is that really my fault? What an odd game, a delusion that time and again confuses the senses and mind so much that one forgets everything that will transpire. What evil force conceals childbirth, procreation, and death behind a fragrant veil of desire? Oh how I tried to escape it. I loved women, so I wouldn't have to love men. It was beautiful, sweet, but the other desire was stronger.

I have so many questions. I've thought so much about this.

I must admit that I envy you. You have your freedom and independence, something I never had. You can develop your talent.

The Immortal One falls silent, her gaze still fixed out the window. Then she finally looks at Berta. I like you, you possess within you something ardent, sincere. Have I frightened you? I have the feeling that I've known you for a long time. Your statue. You know, I can love a work of art like a living being, lose sleep over it, burn and suffer. I thought about how I might be of help to you. Perhaps a commission? I'll try to convince a few friends. Perhaps I could have you do my portrait. What do you think?

I have scores of questions, and I know that I'll never find answers for most of them. I am certain of only one thing: We women must help one another. This is the main thing. We are not raised for friendship the way men are. There is always some ill will between us. We are sisters in misfortune, but we don't conduct ourselves accordingly. Yet we can gain the right to our own lives only through mutual effort. So that someone else's work will not always be placed before our own.

The Immortal One blushes. She gets up, crosses the room,

takes a fan from a dressing table, and begins fanning herself rapidly. She's hot, even though they haven't started heating the apartment and the evenings are still cool. The chambermaid with the vulpine face and piercing eyes removes the coffee cups and then appears with a bottle of brownish liqueur. You must try it, says the woman. Now she's pale again. The girl pours the liqueur into two small glasses and places the bottle on the table. She slams the door as she leaves.

This seems like odd behavior, but the Immortal One just smiles as if amused. She clinks Berta's glass and tosses back the liqueur. It's called *biska*, made in Istria. I learned to drink it on Brijuni, she says, and pours herself some more. It is an astounding island. Have you ever been there? The sunsets, ancient olives, a herd of powerful deer, the glistening of the sea and stars. Lovemaking on dry grass, in sun-warmed coves, in the sand, among the cypresses and ruins of Roman villas. What are your experiences with love, Miss Altmann? Try the liqueur. I imagine that Berlin offers more than Vienna in this regard. I've heard terrible things about Berlin! In Vienna, we only talk about sex. We have some fantasies, but we are afraid to realize them. Apparently, in Berlin it's the opposite. I'm not sure which is better. Perhaps the erotic belongs to the realm of forbidden thoughts, don't you think? A feeling of depravity.

During her speech, she has moved over to the sofa; Berta can feel the soft pressure of her warming thigh and shoulder beneath the silk. She drinks the sweetish liqueur and is surprised at the direction their dialogue has taken. Not a dialogue, thinks Berta, but a monologue. The Immortal One obviously does not expect replies to any of her questions; she sees to the entirety of the discourse herself.

For a moment, Berta becomes lost in thought, and when she comes to in the twilit bedroom, she sees that something has changed. The Immortal One is whispering directly in her face. My poor thing. How they've injured you. I know how it is; I know everything you have suffered and how you suffer still. They've broken your heart. They've taken what's best in you.

She caresses Berta's head, her shoulders, her back.

Berta goes rigid.

Calm down, my dear. Let me caress you; you'll see how beautiful it is. I'll be kind to you, kinder than all the others. We'll drive that pain from your mind. I know just what you need.

Berta is a little tipsy, the room is sinking into darkness, and no one will turn on the lights; no one is coming to save her. It's all a dream, a bad dream. I just have to figure out what it all means is the thought that flashes through Berta's mind when the Immortal One begins to apply force, trying to turn Berta's face and kiss her.

The Immortal One thrusts her tongue into Berta's mouth, presses herself against Berta, unbuttons her blouse, and lifts up her skirt, deftly and quickly, so that Berta is unable to resist.

Berta tries to push the stout woman away with both hands, but it's no use. She feels the woman's hands in her lap and clasps her thighs together. Should she scream? That would be ridiculous. There's a brief knock, then a banging on the door, bright light.

The chambermaid stands at the threshold. Did you ring, ma'am?

Her eyes are inflamed.

She continues, angry and determined: I heard the bell. In any case, the master has arrived and asks how many there will be for supper.

Berta turns to the window. She quickly buttons her blouse and tries to control the laughter rising inside of her.

The Immortal One does not allow herself to be disconcerted.

Some sort of household game into which I've allowed myself to be dragged, thinks Berta. She politely refuses the invitation to supper.

Then it's agreed, says the Immortal One as she accompanies Berta to the door. I'll find you some commissions, trust me. And we'll both mull over my portrait, all right? See how things unfold.

Berta bursts out laughing as she imagines the Immortal One coming to her studio to seduce her. By then she's already standing on the front steps and no one can hear her. When she finally makes it outside, it's dark. She's dizzy after the liqueur and eagerly inhales the fresh autumn air.

If Max were here, he would berate her: You turned her down? Do you realize all the famous people she's had in her bed before you? Then he would begin counting them off. You could have slept with history.

But instead of "slept with," he would use an obscene word.

If he were here, they would have a good laugh.

She won't tell her Viennese friends the story. They wouldn't appreciate the humor of it and would scold her, too. A visit to a class enemy could not turn out otherwise.

CHAPTER 7

Revolution and Departure

THEY DON'T TALK ABOUT CHILDREN. It was one of the conditions Max stipulated before they began living together. He appeared in Berta's studio not even a year after Berta had left him in Berlin. His decision was final; he was not going back to his wife. Only for the sake of his son would he not get a divorce. He was bubbling over with plans. That very day, they went to look at several apartments to rent together, and the reason they finally decided on the one they did was primarily because of its circular room with six high windows. They immediately settled on how to arrange it: with the greatest amount of empty space, cushions in the window recesses, a few lightweight tables. No chairs or even a wardrobe. Colored handwoven curtains. Only later did it occur to Berta that Max hadn't even asked her if she wanted him. She would have said yes, but how could he take it for granted? He attached himself to her entirely, as a matter of course, and even imposed certain conditions: separate bedrooms and no talk of children. Which she accepted. He would travel to Berlin to see his son until he grew up. Then Jo could decide for himself where and with whom he wanted to live.

Four years together—a period of prosperity. The Jauner-Altmann Studio has gradually come to be known as a fashionable atelier. They design a café, a confectioner's, a kindergarten,

134

private homes, and a tennis club. Several pieces of home furniture begin to be produced on a large scale. They have exhibitions in Prague, Budapest, Belgrade. They organize parties, go skiing, and in summer head to the sea. They take a trip to France and Italy. After the economic crisis hits, things slow down a bit, but there's still plenty of work, just badly paid.

Besides designing and fashioning interiors, Berta devotes more and more time to her teaching. She feels better among children than with adults and finds their world endlessly fascinating. When she comes home from her pupils, she is charged with energy and ideas, but as soon as she attempts to place one of them on paper, her certainty vanishes. At the same time, she feels that if she cannot see herself in her artwork, even bad artwork, she won't be able to understand what's happening to her or have any influence on it. Her own art. Not designs, which always have to conform to something, but her own ideas and accomplishments. The white ray. My God, can this really be happening? Could she have imagined back then, years ago, that it would come to this? And to what, in fact, has it come? She's living with Max, something she's always wanted. Max, who doesn't have the slightest recollection of their old prayers. Art means nothing to him. He calls it a bubble, flimflam, a fraud, and makes fun of Berta when she sometimes tries to rebel and defend one of the ideals to which they had once sworn.

The fundamentals of Max's approach to art comprise four points:

One: Everything for the Masses.

Two: The soul and art are bourgeois inventions. Man is an assembly of functions. The idea of self-expression is the same delusion as the notion of creative freedom. No such things exist.

Three: Life is a combination of sugar, carbon, oxygen, starch, and protein. Its quality is determined by exactitude, order, and expedience.

Four: Art is an objective arrangement, exactly corresponding to the organization of the processes of life. It should serve and assist this organization. If it does not, it is without purpose. Everything that is without purpose is worthless.

Above Max's desk hangs a list of life functions that, as an architect of dwelling spaces, he must always keep in mind.

1. Sex life
2. Sleep
3. Pets
4. Gardening
5. Personal hygiene
6. Protection from the weather
7. Housecleaning
8. Automobile maintenance
9. Cooking
10. Heating
11. Sunshine
12. Services

If Berta were to begin painting, it would symbolize a step away from Max, a step more definitive than her escape from Berlin. But it is precisely this step that she cannot take.

Begin at point zero, Paul Klee used to tell them at school. Start by appraising your own position. Where do you stand now? You, just you.

Where does she stand? In a vortex that keeps swirling, ever more rapidly, dangerously, and darkly. She doesn't know where to position the first point, where to direct the line. The only thing she knows is repetition—on the fabric and tapestries she weaves—to repeat the complicated patterns that converge centripetally into her heart, where a reddish, fervid gloom murmurs, where her and Max's nascent children drift away, one by one, in the rivulets of her blood. A spiral unending.

Berta suspects it must someday end, but she cannot imagine how.

Every first Friday of the month, Berta and Max organize a party. After four years, it's become a tradition. Sometimes a new face appears in their circular room, usually a lover of one of their regular guests. The core, however, remains the same.

They listen to music, drink and smoke, and talk about events over the past month. Then Berta serves a simple supper, during which they sit on the floor on cushions. The party ends toward morning with an argument or dancing, depending on how much wine has been drunk and the constellation of friends that has gathered. The most vehement arguments concern politics. In addition to the usual disagreements, a genuinely contentious one has lately arisen: about the new prime minister, Engelbert Dollfuss.

Some are willing to go to blows, claiming that this authoritative Christian Socialist is the only hope in the face of Hitler and the German and Austrian fascists, even if it means using force to introduce order and strengthen Austria's position.

Others assail Dollfuss's actions, in which they see a tendency toward dictatorial aggression and point to his poorly concealed abhorrence of the Left.

A third group is not bothered by a strong hand because it is necessary given the current chaos, but they don't like how Dollfuss is dusting off the Catholic Church, to which he wants to assign the primary role in building a new, self-confident Austria.

Others, Meinlich, for example, overtly refer to him as a fascist.

On the first Friday in December 1932, at eight o'clock in the evening, the phone is ringing in Berta and Max's apartment. It has to ring for a long time.

Jazz is playing on the gramophone, real jazz, the latest thing from New York. One of Berta's girlfriends, recently back from New York, has brought a few records to the party. She talks enthusiastically about America, describing the view of Manhattan with the sharp needles of the skyscrapers, which seem almost to detach themselves and shoot up from the ground; during the day they resemble the rugged cliffs of a smoking volcanic island, and at night they are splashed with insane neon lights and the headlights of an unending series of automobiles gliding along the black asphalt. New York, maddened by the music of thousands of bars, Negro music, and the joyous vitality of dancing bodies. Nowhere in Europe has she seen people exult as the Negroes do in New York when jazz is playing, rhapsodizes her friend. Least of all in Vienna.

Americans are so fast! They move about, assured and single-minded, in a flood of smoke and automobiles. Everything goes like clockwork. No sitting around in cafés, babbling, no metaphysics. Time is money. Perhaps they resemble robots somewhat, said her friend. But they're better equipped for an industrial future than we Europeans, with our oversensitivity and long-windedness. Everything is simpler in America; everything has to function. Problems are solved on the go, and depression is cured with activity. No brooding, but life. You've got to live, baby, sings Berta's friend, kicking out her legs the way she saw the Negroes doing in New York.

In one of the six bay windows, the seats of which Berta has

covered with embroidered cushions, the young left-wing author Eduard Groch is caressing the silk-stockinged leg of a woman who calls herself Salomé, not after the woman who cut off Saint John's head, phooey, but after Freud's famous pupil. She, too, would like to be the lover of Nietzsche or Rilke, write about them, and become famous. Perhaps Groch will be someone, muses the woman, and with this in mind, she allows him to stroke her leg, nothing more.

At the opposite window, the poetess Kurtweil is getting worked up over a book of American psychoanalysis that claims that all women long to be raped—if not physically, at least mentally. This idiot writes that women like to lose! Subconsciously! She can go get stuffed with her subconscious, shouts Kurtweil. She deserves it! There are hundreds of such absurdities in the book, at least two per page. And we're supposed to make progress, when we most enjoy firing into our own ranks!

In his *rubashka* shirt, Meinlich affects disdain, as he does whenever revolution is not the topic of conversation. Today, as usual, he has brought along some poor fellow to get something to eat. The student stuffs himself in silence.

Berta and Max's old friend Ludwig is here, too. Since his return from Paris, he draws nothing but sex organs, detached breasts, and eyes.

The telephone rings for a long time before Berta hears it on the way to the kitchen. The receiver crackles, an intercity call, another crackling, and then the distant voice of Max's wife.

Max comes to the telephone laughing at some joke or other, plugs his other ear so he can hear, a lighted cigarette between his thumb and forefinger.

It's not true, it's not true, it's not true.

Max howls, It's not true, while Berta quickly turns off the gramophone.

She's standing behind Max, ready to shield him.

Max puts down the receiver, turns to Berta, and says, Jo died this afternoon.

That's how it ended. Max went to Berlin and stayed several weeks. He returned to Vienna with his wife, who had collapsed. She felt abandoned, vulnerable; she was afraid of the increasing number of attacks against Jews.

Berta and Max continued working together, but Max never again stayed the night. Jo drew them apart. Berta cannot rid herself of the image of the boy left with only the governess in the large Berlin apartment, how he would turn feverishly to the door, waiting for someone. She knows exactly how Jo felt; the loneliness of her own childhood keeps coming back to her, her illnesses, which she would weep through beneath her covers, convinced that they were leaving her to die. They left Jo to die. Each wrapped up in himself. All the things they professed to do and not do for the sake of Jo, and in the end they let him die.

It was as if she were guilty of boy's death and not his mother, who called the doctor at the very last moment because she was dancing somewhere outside of Berlin while Jo caught cold, then pneumonia, and when the dancer finally arrived, it was too late.

But there's something worse here. Something Berta must forever keep to herself. Several times during these eight long years, at moments when she longed for her own child, she wished for Jo's death. She dreamed about it, what would happen if Jo did not exist.

Sometimes the only thing left is to leave in silence.

After six months, Berta decides to give up her part of the studio. Jauner can continue to use her name. On the surface, nothing will change.

Berta is once again a fugitive. She can't go back to Berlin; Adolf Hitler became the chancellor of the Reich in January, and the Jews are already starting to flee.

She considers Prague. Her aunt on her mother's side lives there, and she has often invited her and offered help. Meinlich, however, restrains her. It would be stupid to leave now that things are starting to happen. In March, Dollfuss dissolved the parliament and declared a state of emergency. In April, he prohibited strikes; in the summer, he banned the Communist Party and the Nazis. He also banned the Republican Guard and ordered them to be disarmed. The workers have had enough; they refuse to listen to Otto Bauer's reassurances anymore. Throughout all of Austria, they are registering and preparing weapons. If they begin police raids and try to make arrests, the workers will defend themselves. They will go on the offensive and assume power. This time, they will not back down. Revolution will be here by winter, claims Meinlich. By winter. But right now, we need every head and every pair of hands, he says.

Why are you so against the Catholic Church? The young man asks Kristýna one fine sunny afternoon. Are you perhaps a Communist? He blushes.

I've never been a Communist.

So why don't you believe in God?

I believe in God

He is confused; for him, God and the Church long ago became one. He contemplates for a moment. But you're a Christian?

Do you mean do I believe that Christ existed?

I mean do you believe that Christ was the son of God? And the Savior.

Yes, in a certain sense.

In what sense?

Can I speak openly with you? she asks.

He nods.

I do not believe in the Resurrection. The idea of the resurrection of the body seems terribly primitive and antiquated to me. As if I believe that Santa Claus brings presents.

He throws up his hands in exasperation: It's not about an idea; it's about dogma.

Precisely.

But to believe, you have to have some sort of foundation, something that cannot be doubted, that cannot be touched. Revealed truth.

Everything must be doubted. Don't you understand? It's the twenty-first century, and you believe in the Resurrection!

He still isn't offended, at least not obviously. He smiles. I'm from this century, miss. It's you who belongs to the past. Look where these doubts have gotten you. Who is supposed to come to the rescue now? With or without faith?

This intrigues Kristýna. Here is someone who thinks that a step backward is actually a step forward.

Look, continues the young man. It is necessary once again to place certain limits on things. Put an end to that individualism of yours, which is basically just the inheritance of eighteenth-century romanticism. This experiment has lasted long enough. We must return to the values upon which our civilization was founded. Before it's too late.

We could also argue about those values, says Kristýna.

What is debatable about love for one's neighbor? Or one must not kill or steal?

Or fornicate. Everyone will sneer at that one.

Why? contends the priest. Isn't AIDS God's punishment?

Kristýna sighs. So an era of fundamentalism is at hand?

Yes, if by this word you mean a return to the fundamentals of faith and not suicides bundled in explosives. What's so bad about that? Who should grasp this if not you, you who experienced the war and forty years of communism? Have you looked at the other side of your freedom? It is swarming with dictators. On the other side of your freedom are gas chambers and concentration camps. The result of your dreams of freedom is the greatest enslavement and subjugation mankind has ever seen. Extremes beget extremes in the other direction. Wouldn't it be better to keep things in proportion? Perhaps with the help of the Church?

But authenticity, personal truth, searching for one's own path, aren't these values?

Not all of us can realize ourselves to the detriment of others. It is time to be done with this outing if anything is still to be preserved.

But I'm an artist, Kristýna says, bringing the conversation to an end, as if that were an explanation.

When the priest leaves, Kristýna continues her reflections. She is not tempted to yield to the calling of the Church, but the conversation has led her to an alarming question: If mankind is really heading in reverse, does that not perhaps prove that man is not internally equipped for freedom?

What if limitations, borders, pressures, violence, which he commits or which he must resist, are his natural environment? Where he is happy. And not in the open, where he soon exhausts himself? What if, consciously and unconsciously, he longs only to be locked up, from the outside or the inside?

A gust of wind, and the sunlight flickers on the yellow hospital wall. A branch brushes against the windowpane. Berta's wonder-struck face: Can you believe I was almost happy in that prison of theirs?

Extremes always go together. In this, the priest was right.

A spontaneous and fragmentary general strike erupted on the afternoon of February 11, an uprising of Austrian workers—or, rather, the armed resistance to state power—on the twelfth. The defense never turned into assault; the protesters didn't even succeed in disturbing the Olympian calm of inner Vienna.

On the radio on the afternoon of the twelfth, the prime minister read a speech, in which he reassured the citizens of Vienna that the situation was under control. The Bolshevik Revolution, or whatever it was supposed to be, had collapsed, and no further skirmishes were imminent. Then they broadcast a waltz from *Der Rosenkavalier*. At around the same time, the army began firing on the workers' tenement complex Karl Marx-Hof.

Conflicts continued in several places in Vienna until the fifteenth, and the government suppressed the report of three hundred dead. Berta was arrested the morning of the sixteenth in the apartment of Robert Meinlich.

Robert's landlady, the old widow Rosenbaum, opened the door for Berta as usual and let her in without a word. She looked distraught and close to tears, but Berta suspected nothing. Lots of people had been crying in Vienna over the past three days.

She didn't even ask if Meinlich was home; if he hadn't been, Rosenbaum wouldn't have let her in. She knocked smartly on the glass pane of the door to his room and entered without waiting for an invitation. She had dutifully walked into a trap and even closed the door behind her. Robert was not in the room; instead, four unidentified men surrounded her and announced she was under arrest for suspicion of preparing an insurrection.

Hands on the table, sweaty palm prints. Her face reflected in the polished tabletop. Angry, humiliated, frightened, of course, but at the same time relieved. Her situation has never been clearer. She's the prisoner, the one being interrogated. Unable to leave or even stir. Her pain and her internal confusion have suddenly died away before the shiny, bloated face of the man who alternately shouts at her and then speaks in a kind, fatherly voice.

They won't get anything from her because she doesn't know anything. She doesn't know where Meinlich disappeared to. She doesn't know what further activities the Party is planning, or even what contact her organization had with Otto Bauer. Apparently, Bauer has fled to Bratislava. Today, Dollfuss outlawed the Social Democrats as well as every other party except his own.

She's a teacher, she keeps repeating. She teaches the children of workers. Do you have anything against art history? Is gluing together collages and drawing still lifes a subversive activity? Do the workers not have a right to education?

You're either naive or disingenuous. He waves one of her agitprop posters in front of her face. His face is yellow. She senses violence in his voice and a desire to strike her. She starts to tremble. Afraid she'll start crying, she feels pitiful. She would most like to crawl beneath the table and beg him to spare her. To control herself, she fixes her attention on the black typewriter, counting the keys, the pearl-edged round buttons with a silver letter in the center. In her mind, she assembles them into patterns. She observes that the clock is slightly askew. The room loses its usual dimensions, closing in, doused in a poisonous green-and-yellow crapulence. The inspector gets up, walks around the table, and now starts shouting at her from behind for a change. He leans over and breathes on her neck. He had sausage and onions for lunch. Her stomach rises.

Okay, one more time. You're really starting to worry me. I wouldn't want to have to be severe with you.

He returns to her field of vision and sits down on his chair with a groan.

Berta thinks his liver is bothering him.

At the end of the interrogation, they write up the minutes, he gives them to her to sign, and a young policeman leads her to a cell.

That's how it goes, day after day.

During the interrogations, Max's name comes up several times, even the name of his wife. Apparently, they paid Mr. Jauner a visit at his home. It's strange. They have nothing on Max, who was much more active in the Party than Berta. They ascribe all of his political activity to her, the immoral, corrupt, unprincipled, unmarried, and childless Bolshevik Berta Altmann. Basically, a whore.

If he had a daughter like that, he would disown her, the investigator confides at one point. It's a good thing her parents didn't live to experience this disgrace.

After four days, they let her go but with a warning. She is to watch herself. She's on a list of people under surveillance. One false step could be fatal.

For now, the battle for Austria is lost: Fascism has won. Many people around me claim it's not fascism and that Dollfuss's dictatorship is the only possible defense against the German Nazis or the Bolsheviks (whom they fear more than Hitler). A lesser evil, that's something that doesn't interest me. I returned to Vienna—a place I really didn't want to be—so I could be of use somehow. I didn't give speeches at meetings. I didn't want to spill anyone's blood. Art is a path toward the light, to the emancipation of man; this is something I believe in, something for which I'm willing to sacrifice everything. Now I'm done with teaching; the inspector made that quite clear. I'm no longer allowed to do anything in this police state. Yet another reason to go elsewhere. People have been fleeing Germany for some time now. Everyone says that Prague is safe for the time being, and refugees are treated well. Perhaps I could get citizenship; if I wanted to go farther to the west, it would be easier with a Czechoslovak passport. I don't know. Max is staying here. For now. I still have to talk to him. He has to explain to me this sudden change that's come over him and why he suddenly distanced himself from our group. Why he got scared. Or is he avoiding me? I haven't seen him for a good six months.

At one point, the investigator asked me why I was a Communist. And why we wanted to confiscate and destroy everything no matter what.

We don't want to destroy, I said. On the contrary, we want to create a world in which people will be able to live according to their actual abilities and where they will not be condemned to poverty and inferiority just because they were born into a certain social class. We want everyone to have enough food and heat, so they don't have to choose between working for money and working for the soul.

And you believe that rigmarole about the nobility of poverty? the inspector said, lighting into me. I wish you could see what I saw when I was a patrolman. No such thing exists, believe me. Nobility occurs only in people who can afford it. As soon as you give in to the rabble, they will rob and slaughter us all. Don't you know what happened in Russia after the Revolution?

If you give people what they need, they will change, I told him.

They will never change. He shook his head.

I believe in people, I said.

I could have saved myself this lecture. The reason I joined the Communists is actually more straightforward. I could have become a Sister of Mercy in the same way if I believed in God. It's that stab of pain, that clenching in my gut whenever I witness poverty or degradation or illness. All I have to do is pass a beggar on the street on a beautiful sunny day, and all that beauty is gone. I experience his pain, his degradation as my own. In Berlin, I saw college professors handing out shoelaces on the street. I saw workers, who had supported themselves their entire lives through honest work, abasing themselves and begging. I will never forget their faces. Degradation is worse than poverty. Degrading even for the one giving alms. For a few pennies, the one who happens to be spared purchases a tranquil conscience and at the same time the feeling that nothing like this could ever befall him.

I cannot; I may not live only for myself. I don't have money; I have nothing to sacrifice but my time and my energy.

But even so, I am plagued by doubts. Is my teaching really good for something, or am I merely trying to convince myself? No, I am not. Art assuages and illuminates their lives; it elevates them from the everyday, grueling banality, the dirt, the struggle for basic necessities. I myself know well enough how grueling this struggle is! And how much happiness a flash of beauty, of color, of understanding, a glimpse of another world can give someone who trudges day after day with his eyes fixed on the tips of his shoes. I want to believe that this experience can lead them further, like a lucky star. Especially a child. Children, who are still not worn down, who still have not lost touch with their fantasy. A good teacher can change their lives completely. Redirect them, save them, keep them from getting stuck and foundering in unhappiness. Nothing is more persistent, tenacious than poverty! Art is not an ivory tower. It is an escape, but not into illusion. It is a stepladder to higher tiers of human consciousness, to brighter, happier levels of life. The teacher teaches how to place one's feet on higher and higher rungs without falling. Each new rung represents another step out of hell and expands the field of possibilities. At every rung, an obstacle disappears, the vicious circle is broken, and one internal block crumbles away. It's a miracle: the flowering beneath my hands, the blossoming. A good teacher liberates. I want to believe I have this ability.

Maybe I'm too good a teacher to accomplish anything in art myself. What if art and teaching are mutually exclusive? Question: Must one really work and scrape by only for oneself to be able to create something? Must one be self-centered? Or is this just another myth? There must be some other way. In any case, a woman cannot create like this. She cannot close herself off with what she has, isolate herself, transform herself into some kind of monument. If she does, her power evaporates or turns against her. A woman must fight her way through from the opposite direction: open herself up more and more, make of herself a transit station and take it to the verge of her own effacement, allow herself to be harvested and devoured, dissolve in generosity. Perhaps a woman creates less, but more deeply, and she always gives more.

I go through life immersed in myself, in my fears and frustrations, and this paralyzes me. I am not connected by all my roots, I do not absorb with all my mouths, and the exchange of nutrients between myself and the universe does not proceed as effortlessly and fluently as it should. I am like an oyster that must be opened with a knife. This knife is a child.

I long to give more than I am able!

And there's something else I should have said to the investigator: As long as there is compassion among people, there will be communism. Or something like it. What a paradox: They condemn communism, and at the same time their mouths are full of Jesus.

Everywhere they are now swearing by the people and the Catholic Church!

In the Botanical Garden

He stands beneath a lone sycamore tree; footpaths branch out beneath his feet in all four directions. A hat sits atop his head, and the collar of his overcoat is turned up against the wind and rain. Hands in pockets. Max never wears gloves. How many pairs has she bought him, and sooner or later, a week at most, he always loses one. He's looking the other way.

Max always used to wait for her eagerly, turned in the direction opposite from which she was coming. He did not sense her in the distance as she did him; she was not a magnet toward which he would rotate, even in his sleep. Wrong. It is in sleep he would most likely find her. Awake, he placed between himself and her, between himself and everyone else, a host of obstacles.

Perhaps it's because Max tries to interpret, understand, and make sense of everything. Everything that comes his way, he takes apart and wraps up into tidy packages with a label. As if he is pushing life away from himself with his head.

He's explained to himself the death of his son. He's been

going to psychoanalytic sessions for the past six months and feels discernibly stronger, armed with an entire battery of new terminology that can be felicitously deployed. His relief is in being able to create an intelligible account of himself.

He feels better; he no longer wakes up in the middle of the night in anguish. He doesn't even miss Berta that much, since the doctor has helped him understand his dependency on her and has given a name to the role Berta played in his life. It was high time to free himself from her and finally grow up. He still lives with his wife, but even that relationship cannot be saved. There's nothing bad in this, nothing he should reproach himself for, Dr. Hauschke told him. Such relationships are merely peripeteia in the drama of searching for oneself.

He feels better; there's no doubt about that. He's even working again.

But through some sort of crevice, perhaps in those places where the doctor's interpretations do not quite fit, Max feels as if sadness is trickling into him. Flowing in, then flowing out, peacefully, without surprise, just as all his days now are without surprise. Such a subtle outflow of energy, low pressure. The inability to deceive himself, to be inspired by something. A state of sobriety.

He often thinks about death. Not with passion, heroism, rapture, and even gratefulness as before. He sees it merely as the crude and unjust end of the body. His body, the only possible bearer of the consciousness designated by the name Max Jauner, is moving through space toward its end. This is called time.

He does not fear death in general, but he is afraid of his own death. Perhaps it is death that has deprived Max's world of its former radiance.

Berta approaches from the Belvedere. She recognizes his

back between the bare bushes, unusually wide in his dark winter coat.

Wet gravel sticks to her shoes.

Max Jauner!

He turns toward her voice. She sees his delicate feline face. He smiles, and his eyes resemble those of a boy.

Berta Altmann!

Max Jauner! She goes over and takes him by the hands, which are damp and warm from being in his pockets. She presses herself against him. They embrace for a long time, firmly; they apprehend each other through the layers of coats and sweaters; they sense every bone, joint, cushion of flesh. The imprints of trilobites.

When they pull themselves apart, Berta is wiping away tears.

Max Jauner, she says again, laughing.

Berta Altmann. He takes her arm.

I need to sit down. Her legs are trembling.

They sit down on a bench along an avenue of chestnuts.

They are silent. Together.

Max wants to tell her a lot of things. Explain to her why he has decided to stay in Vienna while so many of their mutual friends are leaving. Explain to her the reasons he has finally placed his trust in Dollfuss and his politics, despite the tragedy that has occurred. He wants to explain why his fervor for revolution has been fading lately, that it is connected to his loss of faith in the ideal person. He believes only in that which he can achieve immediately himself. Great words resound with emptiness. Perhaps this change came about with the death of Jo. Perhaps it was his conversations with people who came back from Russia shaken by how the rule of the people looks in practice. He wants her to believe him. He's already experienced one slaughter firsthand and feels another is being prepared, perhaps much worse than the first. Only men like Dollfuss can accomplish something here. The times are primitive, barbarous; they will allow only the strongest to survive, a leader with a clear concept, with the courage to amputate the invalid's arm. It is necessary to rip the sentimentality from everyone, even the compassion. People must think concretely from day to day. And, in the first place, act before others do.

He needs to tell her all of that. Instead, he is just silently absorbing the warmth radiating from the being next to him, from her hand.

But the moment lengthens, too much for Jauner's restless mind: How long is Berta going to sit here like this? he wonders. What time is she actually leaving? Is her luggage at the train station?

Are you going to accompany me to the gate? asks Berta suddenly. But no farther.

They get up and slowly walk along the white, wet, sticky gravel.

We'll definitely see each other soon, says Jauner. I'll write you.

Berta says nothing.

After a few steps, she says, Don't write for now. I'll write you myself.

Soon?

When I forget about you, Berta thinks, although does not say this. She nods.

Berta—Max suddenly stops and turns her to face him so he can look into her eyes—you're not running away from me, are you? It's not my fault you're leaving, is it?

You know why I'm running away. I don't want to be in this country, and you have nothing to do with it.

Be happy, Berta, I beg you!

I probably don't know how.

Unhappiness is like an illness.

No one can cure me of fate.

At least promise me you'll try.

I promise.

Are you sure you don't want me to go with you to the train station?

I'm sure.

At the gate to the botanical garden, they embrace once again. It's a depleted drawing near of bodies; they're no longer together. Berta walks away quickly.

Berta! This is what he has wanted to say, and he does now: We didn't lose, did we?

She stops. Looks at him, vigilant, anxious. Lose what? What do you mean by that? How have we lost?

Max doesn't know. Was it love, art, politics? There was so much.

Berta was hoping for something else: a miracle, a sudden insight that would change Max's view of her and allow her to return. They would go to Prague together and start a new life there, a new Berta and a new Max, forget about the bad things. After all, who else but she could comfort Max and bring him back him to life? She was mistaken. She understands the thin, perplexed smile on Max's face.

Once more she embraces him, caresses his back, the nape of his neck, the hair beneath his hat, and tells him what he wants to hear: Everything will be fine. She will not abandon him. She will always love him. He will never be alone. He is extraordinary and will achieve great things even without her.

Only then does she go.

A diminutive, dark, moving figure in the white symmetry of

the park, past the dried-up fountain, down the chestnut avenue toward the metal gate.

Max does not wait for Berta to go out onto the busy street. He returns to the botanical garden, wanders among the rock gardens in a state of peculiar intoxication. He no longer feels anxiety, or remorse. How strong Berta is, how powerful, he says to himself. Remarkably strong and courageous.

Milena is reading about Israel. The author of one of the books claims that the battle between the Jews and the Arabs is merely a continuation of Word War II because every injustice is carried further and balanced out with another injustice. That's history: an unbroken chain of violence, an overflow of power, and an alternation of roles between the usurpers and usurped. Genuine peace would mean their interruption. But such peace is not possible, just as absolute forgiveness is not possible. The screaming of the murdered is carried upon its echo; spilled blood calls out for more blood. The transgressor never becomes the victim; instead, some third party does.

Every culpable deed is everlasting, writes the author, passed down from generation to generation, persisting in the thoughts of the coercers and the coerced and deforming their perception of the world.

Guilt and the longing for power, those are the two motive forces that drive the wheel of history.

Let us follow attentively, without self-deception, the universal dynamic of violence, exhorts the author. And we shall see that our prospects for the future are not exactly rosy.

Politics had never interested Milena, but ever since she started thinking about Aaron, she has bought a newspaper every day. Anxiously, she looks for news about suicide attacks, which, after a long period of calm, have begun to appear with appalling regularity.

Another book says that the biblical Promised Land is actually a prison—for both the Palestinians and the Jews. Who is the warden and who the prisoner? And does it matter? The author analyzes the psychology of the victim and wonders how much time will pass before the centuries of persecution and World War II will be erased from the collective memory of the Jews. How long are we going to feel sorry for ourselves and look upon ourselves as the menaced and afflicted while we menace and afflict the other? When will we succeed in freeing ourselves from our own past?

Milena imagines Aaron beneath the desert sun, in the light that strips and lays everything bare, where weak passions, hesitant dreams, melancholy, delicate hues do not thrive. She dreams of Jerusalem at night. A city where the moon is larger and more powerful, suspended low in the sky. The bloody moon, a pungent fragrance, curtains of darkness. Sweetness, quiescence. Craggy rocks exude the moisture sucked deep from the earth. The pulse of blood, the babel and burgeoning of the darkness. Oh, to submerge oneself in its fleece!

She sees Aaron exhausted by the sun, seeking shade.

If anything happens to Aaron, she will not even know.

CHAPTER 8

Prague

WHAT WAS PRAGUE LIKE in the middle of April 1934? Blossoming, old, crumbling. Charming, more so than Vienna, than any city Berta has ever visited. She sees in Prague several cities at once, each overlapping the other.

Berta perceives Prague as ancient compared to the rest of Czechoslovakia, where everything still has the atmosphere of novelty and personal enthusiasm.

In Prague, the Czechs try to assist refugees from Germany and Austria; they organize collections, invite them to their homes, and find them work. They're proud they can admit them to their country and provide protection.

The immigrants, among whom Berta has encountered several previous acquaintances from Berlin and the Weimar school, which the Nazis already managed to close, meet regularly in the studio of the painter K. He was among the first to relocate to Prague and, despite the economic crisis, succeeded in building up a fairly good network of acquaintances. He has his own art dealer, paints portraits of well-known personalities, and gives private lessons. He himself is not politically active, but his studio on the banks of the Moldau is an active center of anti-Nazi and anti-fascist activity.

With the help of Communist émigrés and their Czech

friends, Berta manages to find a position as an art teacher at a
Prague school. In the fall, she and another woman from Vienna
rent a small apartment in Prague-Nusle, and she moves out of
her aunt's place.

Her reacquaintance with the figurative, tenaciously Expres-
sionist work of the painter K. has contributed to Berta's confi-
dence. Her first completed painting is called *The Interrogation*.

The woman with her back to the viewer is her. The only
things visible are her dark, hunched back, shoulders, the crown
of her head, and her bright red earlobes. The investigator's face
is a yellowish green. He is leaning on the desk with one knotty
fist while the other pounds on the typewriter keys, which look
so real that they seem glued to the painting. The round ivory
buttons with their clearly visible letter in the center. Time hangs
askew on the wall in the shape of pendulum clock from the
time of Franz Josef.

In October 1934, Berta meets a young artist named Milan
Drůza at the Artists' Union. She is introduced by Kristýna
Hládek, whom Berta knows from the painter K.'s studio. Milan
is four years younger than Berta. He's interested in his Austrian
colleague primarily because she studied at the Weimar school
during the time of its greatest glory.

Their tête-à-tête continues past midnight, and Milan insists
on walking Berta home. It's almost morning when they reach
Nusle from Malá Strana, but Berta doesn't mind if Milan comes
in.

She makes a pot of strong coffee with sugar. They sit together
in the paling darkness and continue their conversation, quietly,
so they don't wake Greta, who is asleep in the next room. All
at once, the remote corner of the room blushes, turns red, then
orange. The radiance travels across the room, alights on the
mirror, the painting on the wall, Milan's face. Morning jostles

into the room through a gap in the curtains. They observe each other smiling. How long have they actually known each other? Berta gets up and with a brusque movement shifts the curtain, freeing up the window. Not a trace of the fiery radiance. The dull autumn sunlight peers into the room serenely. The luminous clear sky traverses the Nusle roofs. The spidery sky, says Berta.

Her companion looks fresh, as if he has just awakened from a good sleep and not stayed up with her all night. When he finally gets up to say good-bye, Berta looks him over properly for the first time. He looks strong and healthy, not very tall, but with wide shoulders and a warm palm, which swallows up Berta's hand entirely and then some. His light, curly hair is already giving intimations of a bald spot as it clambers up his temples and recedes past his forehead. His round, open face with its expressive crooked nose and clear blue eyes. Soft pink lips. Berta knows they are soft because before his departure he kisses her right cheek, then her left, and then once again her right, like in Paris. In Paris, they kiss three times, he says, and smiles.

Even in the morning, he smells slightly of cologne.

It's Saturday and Berta doesn't have to go anywhere. After Milan leaves, she climbs into bed, bundles up into the warm blanket, and purrs. In Paris, they kiss three times. Hmm, hmm, hmm.

It's been a long time since she's felt so good. She finds herself on smooth rails slipping along safely to sleep. In Paris. Oh yes.

I started going to see Dr. Mahler. Greta arranged it for me because she says she can't bear to see me suffer any longer. After a few sessions, I have the sense that my case (I'm a case!!!) is nothing special whatsoever. It seems there are thousands of such unfortunate crackpots like me dashing about the world.

The heart of the problem, says the doctor, obviously has its roots in childhood. I never would have guessed, I said to Greta, but my irony upset her. She says I'll never be cured like that.

Dr. Mahler looks trustworthy. He has such a classically fatherly face—graying mustache, imperial beard, and a high forehead. During our sittings—or rather, lyings—I can't see him; he sits in an armchair with his back to the window. A dark silhouette with a deep, pleasant voice. Behind my head. I'm on the sofa. (Berta Altmann on a psychoanalyst's sofa! Maja would have exploded with laughter.)

I recount—or rather, blab—whatever comes into my head, while he mostly remains silent. Only now and then does he pose a few follow-up questions. At the end, he sums up the entire séance, explains how far we've gotten that day and how it might (it doesn't have to) relate to my problems.

It seems my father interests him the most. Whenever I mention him, he suddenly seems to wake up. I practically hear him turning the pages of Freud in his head. But stop it. Hush, Berta! You'll never get anywhere like this. And there's nothing left but to remain alone, all alone, and sob at night beneath the covers so that Greta doesn't hear you.

Now I must write down what the doctor and I have concluded.

We've reduced my problems to three fundamental obstacles: a powerful feeling of guilt, a distrust of my surroundings, especially of people who manifest good-will toward me, and an inability to finally begin to live (paint) the way I really want to and the way I feel. That is: Do I really know what I want? That's what it is. I feel that I've always done and continue to do many things only because other people want me to. I have always conformed because I've been afraid of losing someone. And now? The only thing Milan wants is that I not resist his love. And what am I doing? Secretly thinking about escape.

The doctor surmises that, in view of my lonely and unhappy childhood, I'm always seeking the love and acceptance of those around me. At the same time, I do not believe they could accept me the way I really am. Thus I try with all my might to adapt. I am shackled by my longing for love, and I dare not do anything that might displease someone. This is the real reason I hesitate in my painting. Because of the way I see the world, my vision, my kind of talent, my sensibility, everything pulls me in a direction that was not and is not popular with people around me. I am always the first to condemn myself. But when I want to work in concert with my mind, with my conviction of how modern art should look, I idiotically start to imitate others.

The doctor and I also talked about my friends, Milan and the painter K. The latter helped me a great deal when I arrived in Prague. He says (and keeps repeating) that art is not about talent, not even craft. It is merely the courage to do what you really want and need to do. It is about finding your own expression, in spite of the times, generally accepted taste, and all manner of pressures. With his own art, he proves it's possible. He has never painted an abstract in his life. He says it doesn't interest him; it, in fact, bores him. His interest in a subject, the begin-ning of the process of painting, always commences with an external form that enchants him: color, form, coarseness or softness, a gleam in the eyes. The material—behind which he perceives something eternal. Through painting he reveals, x-rays, brings to the surface what is inside. But the surface remains. He can disturb it, break it up, scarify it, but never abstract it. Art is not abstraction, but penetration to the heart, beholding the terrible and marvelous averted faces. Stratification. The image must be richer than the gaze. Not poorer. Abstraction is the child of the idea and as such is always merely an impoverishment.

I cannot agree with him entirely, but I know what he means. I, too, am attracted to painting primarily by surfaces, light, the pleasure of the gaze, the desire to capture, freeze an instant. I, too, enjoy telling stories of people and things instead of points, colors, and lines. But perhaps this depends rather on the temperament, the makeup of the person. I don't think abstract painters— Paul Klee, for example—do anything essentially different from what K. does. The difference is that K. (like me) is corporeal, robust, full-blooded. And Paul is Song of the Blue Tree.

My thoughts often turn to Paul. He's in Switzerland and apparently afflicted with some rare illness. My God, I hope he is not in pain! The idea that this kindhearted, gentle man is suffering is terrible.

But back to K. I told the doctor that one day I worked up my courage and took my painting <u>The Interrogation</u> to him. He is the greatest authority I know here in Prague. To my surprise he praised it. But he also said I was only at the very beginning of seeking my own expression. I must continue and not let myself be discouraged by anything. I must follow every manifestation of myself, even if it seems *banal or stupid. Because it is precisely that which will show me how to continue.*

He more or less said, You are a rich and interesting individual who is trying to squeeze into a form that doesn't suit you. You're afraid to be yourself and therefore you don't know who you are. But to become something, you must find it first. You must paint images that are you. Exactly like you. Paint with everything! With all of your imperfections! With everything you do not like in yourself. Paint with your sexual energy! Take the plunge. And don't listen to anyone, least of all me.

That's what the painter K. said to me, not Dr. Mahler.

Dr. Mahler just confirmed for me that half my life I've been a slave to my desire to be loved.

What a paradox, I said to the doctor. I want to be loved and at the same time I'm not capable of believing that someone could love me.

It's simply the other side of the same coin, he replied. You were tied up for too long in a relationship that essentially mimicked your relationship with your father. You were in love with someone who did not love you enough. You recognize this pattern in which you feel safe. When there's a danger that you must change something, you get scared. That's normal. You're reluctant to step into unfamiliar territory.

So what should I do?

The doctor threw up his hands, as if surprised that it hadn't long been obvious. Leap. Have the courage to be loved, with all the risks it entails. Happiness requires courage. So have the courage, he told me.

It's interesting that K. said almost exactly the same thing: Paint, taking all of the risks.

But to do that, first of all I would have to be rid of myself. Because am I entitled to happiness? Do I, in fact, not deserve further suffering, further punishment?

The doctor claims that I must separate my subjective guilt from its external causes. For those are merely justifications connected with my feeling of guilt only in my imagination.

The need to feel guilt was present before anything else, said Mahler. Even were your life completely perfect, your need to experience guilt would seek out and find ever more forms. Thus first of all, you must stop tormenting yourself because of something, so to speak, external and look into the torment itself. Torment is a process. How does it arise? What is it feeding on?

The doctor said (approximately, I don't remember the exact words), Let me suggest the following hypothesis, but I must emphasize that you do not have to accept it in the least.

What if this relatively simple circumstance were at the root of your feelings of guilt: A child feels abandoned, lacking attention and an ample quantity of love. She cannot blame her parents, for this would be an unbearable blow. The faultlessness of one's parents is the only certainty one can rely on. So what does the child do? She blames her negative feelings on herself. Later, when she grows a little older, she establishes the real culprit. Perhaps she even starts to hate her parents and completely forgets that at one time she condemned herself. But the initial condemnation persists in her as a feeling of guilt. Forgotten and all the more insidious. It returns and grows stronger with every internal setback: I am responsible for everything. It's my fault. I am not good enough and cannot be good.

Finally, concluded Dr. Mahler, the victim of such self-hatred purposely seeks out failures because only in them does she feel at home, safe. Even if at the same time she longs for happiness, like everyone else. But safety and certainty of habit are often a stronger enticement than the vague fantasy of happiness. Keep that in mind. One can even get used to suffering and somehow survive within it.

What should I conclude from this? I think it over. But I can't think too long, or Milan will change his mind. Should I leap? How many more opportunities will I have?

Milan is patient and so good that it exceeds all measure of understanding. There's nothing complicated in him; he doesn't possess Max's captiousness and skepticism. When he sets off somewhere, he does not doubt he'll get there. No other possibility occurs to him. He's completely external, round, smooth; everything he touches lights up and grows warm.

I warm myself against him, recuperate. Because he wants me, I want to kiss his feet. Because he does not flee before the problems that I drag around with me. You are an enchanted princess, he tells me, but one kiss is not enough. There must be many, many more. An entire river! If only I could purify myself in it and wash away the hurts of the past fifteen years. To be young and fresh, capable of hope, trust, happiness. For him.

A ruddy male body on a yellow bedspread, the color of skin and ocher (a naked body thrown in clay), a body spread out on Berta's bed, prone, the face buried in the pillow. The skin of the shoulders glistens dimly. The hair on his head and light clumps of hair on his arms, thighs, and calves emit a weak glow in the rays of sun entering through the open door to the entrance hall.

A lance of sunlight is thrust through the apartment from the kitchen to Berta's room, pulling a cord of light through the Nusle apartment building.

Milan glistens and sleeps.

Berta sits in her wing-backed chair, which followed her from Berlin to Vienna and then to Prague. With her legs tucked beneath her, wrapped in a light robe, she emits golden spirals of smoke. On her knees lies a sketchbook, her pencil quickly flashing along the paper. Moving as if by itself, magnetized by Berta's gaze.

The wedding takes place in the spring of 1936 in Prague's Old Town Hall. Berta becomes Altmann-Drůzová and a Czechoslovak citizen. In letters to friends, she leaves off the little circle above the *u,* as well as the Czech suffix *–ová.*

For their honeymoon, they go to the spa town Lázně Luhačovice, where Berta undergoes a therapeutic cure. The doctor recommended it after her last miscarriage. She is thirty-six years old. No longer young. The gynecologist said, You are no longer a young woman. After the age of thirty-five, the probability of becoming pregnant decreases sharply. And there's your past, all those abortions. We'll do what we can, but I if I were you, I wouldn't place any great store by it.

> *I am standing at the window of my Prague apartment, looking out: down at the tracks and the little booth of the train station. My canvas is fastened to the easel. I paint. If they saw me at school, I'd be laughed at. They wouldn't believe their eyes. We used to burn easels! We never wanted to paint from life. We didn't want to lie. From the window! I am standing in my living room and painting what I see. I become the tracks, the train station, the reddish reflection on the roof of the building opposite. I wander.*

I cease to be that anxious, burdened woman. Like this, I feel calm, untroubled. I do not want to look within, but without.

I paint from the window. I can do no more. I cannot. In this "I cannot" is a truth that makes it possible for me to paint. I am she who cannot. I shake off the tyranny of success. The tyranny of words: quality, selection, function. The tyranny of programs and proclamations, ideas, ideals, decrees for what should be instead of what is.

I proclaim myself inferior, nonfunctional, nonpowerful. I pronounce myself to be everything I was not allowed to be. I say, I cannot, I cannot, and at the same time I feel a reluctant but distinct influx of courage.

I did not want to be anything but free, moans Kristýna. I destroyed everything behind me, freed myself from everything. I thought to myself that now, in peace, I would prepare myself for death. I can finally stand aside, be selfish. Meanwhile, everything is hurtling down on me. It began with those film people, whom I should have tossed out, and it's getting worse and worse, as if someone were mocking me. Everything is pulling me downward and backward: memories, my body, and Milena, who comes here threatening to leave for Israel because she doesn't know how to live in Prague. Why Israel? What is she looking for?

Kristýna's hip is not healing. After a few rehab sessions, she had to stop exercising. She couldn't take the pain. The doctors wanted to send her home; they say she's depriving other younger patients of space. But then her fevers started again, and her leg began to swell. The x-rays showed something wrong, the joint had not set properly. They will have to operate again, said the head physician, or immobilize the leg. Then the pain would not be so great, but Kristýna would never walk again. They asked her son if he would agree to the operation. At Kristýna's age, any anesthesia is life-threatening, and if the operation is not absolutely necessary, it should be avoided. They didn't ask her; obviously, they don't consider her competent. In the end, however, she had to decide for herself because Mirek broke down under the stress of responsibility; he came straight from the doctor to tell her everything—in tears.

Don't go crying about me, she said. If you haven't noticed, I'm quite alive and well. Go ahead and sign the paper. No anesthesia is going to lay me out, I can promise you that. She pretended to be cheerful and preferred exiting under anesthesia to living in pain as a cripple. Besides, it would be quite a fine death. Mirek believed her—he always snatches at anything she offers—went away calm, and signed the doctor's release.

She cannot halt the stream of memories, which violently thrust themselves into her consciousness. The past returns even in her dreams, and the other two women in the room start to complain. Kristýna doesn't allow them to sleep in peace; she talks to someone throughout the night. It's all quite incomprehensible and sounds like mumbling or groaning, which is worse than snoring.

Father Dominik, who is still coming to see Kristýna, offers her confession. Even though she refuses to believe in God's mercy and forgiveness, she could feel relief, he tells her. The greatest suffering arises from a person being alone with his black thoughts.

She's attracted to the idea of telling this young man things she's always kept to herself. Who else could she consider? She can't speak with her son about it, not even with Milena. Children should have at least a somewhat ideal conception of their parents and grandparents. Their own lives are then all the more pleasant.

During another visit from Father Dominik, Kristýna cautiously returns to the idea of confession. Has he changed his mind? I must warn you, she says, I have a great many sins.

Pride, he says, raising his finger. Have you ever been to confession?

Never.

Are you telling me you've never once in your life, even as a little child, confessed your sins and received absolution?

No. So where do I begin?

Begin with the Lord.

I've never done Him any wrong.

The priest sighs deeply. Begin where you want.

In town, I met Kristýna Hládek, that young artist who introduced us to Milan. She had even been at our wedding. Apparently, he had tried to make a sexual advance, just like all the men around, but now, naturally (!), she no longer interests him in that way.

At first, I misunderstood (we were speaking Czech). She hadn't come back from Paris but, on the contrary, wanted to go there as soon as possible.

She's awfully talkative and direct. She followed me all the way across Charles Square, calling out, Mrs. Altmann! Berta! Until people started to turn and stare. She kept saying she wanted to see my artworks and how she would love to visit us, until I finally invited her for Sunday. She appeared quite excited.

She doesn't seem conceited to me at all, unlike what people say about her. She behaved just like a little girl with me. She's very pretty, a real beauty. I'm not surprised Milan likes (liked) her. Even I almost fell in love with her—innocently, of course. I've clarified this aspect of myself long ago, after my visit with the Immortal One. I am able to admire the allure of women; I find it inspiring and erotic, but not in a sexual way.

Kristýna is tall and slender, with narrow hips like a boy's. She has a mane of marvelous red hair, all ringlets, and a perfectly oval face, somewhat pale, with a delicate, thin nose, dark, high eyebrows, and childlike lips. Like a Renaissance Madonna.

She said she'd just passed the entrance exams in textile design at the Academy of Applied Arts. According to her, the professors there are better than at the Academy of Fine Arts. (Why is that always the case?) But she still wants to continue painting. She asked if I wanted to teach her.

You're no longer studying with the painter K.? I asked.

She blushed and stammered that, no, she wouldn't be going to see him anymore.

But now to the main thing: War has broken out in Spain! The fascists have attacked the leftist government, which won the elections in the spring. It's a conspiracy by one part of the army and the Church; at least that's how I understood it. All of the world's progressive forces, democrats, Communists, socialists, anarchists, even those simply on the side of human dignity, freedom, and justice vocally support the Republicans. The rest are backing the insurgents. The rest—that means MONEY.

Money is once again committing murder, this time in Spain. With the official support of England, France, and primarily Germany, of course, which has sent its airplanes and professional army. They are bombing villages, killing unarmed people, children. I've read and heard terrible things! In Spain, thousands of people are dying, defenseless, for our cause. There they are fighting against Hitler,

Dollfuss, Mussolini! Apparently, a lot of German Jews are fighting in the international brigades alongside the English, the French, the Italians, even the Americans! And it's not only Communists. It's not a matter of nationality or even political conviction. These people are fighting against fascism. They are voluntarily going to their deaths so that dogmatism, exploitation, persecution, and book burning do not prevail.

Many of my acquaintances welcome this development. They say it is high time the two poles of the world stand against each other in a decisive battle that will show which is stronger. They do not doubt our victory because they say the people are on our side. And the people always require war in order to rise up and move forward, like in the Soviet Union in 1917. They say that a new order will emerge from this war. But why must the innocent die for it?

I have the insistent feeling that I must do something; I cannot just look on. My own work has once again ceased. I cannot disengage, close my eyes and ears, and do my own work, invent, paint. Perhaps I could have been an artist in another century, but unfortunately I was born in the twentieth. What are we doing? We organize financial collections for fugitives and victims of the war. We write letters asking for help. We try to explain ourselves, to spread awareness of what is happening in Spain and why.

Art during a time of revolution is not a calling or a profession, but a neurosis. Where did I read that?

Every now and then, Berta returns from a walk with some stray dog. They join her of their own accord. So far none has stayed, but she suspects it's only a matter of time before an owner doesn't show up and she'll have a dog. She doesn't want to acquire one herself. She's afraid to shackle an animal to herself merely for her own enjoyment. It would be better if it came by itself.

She still lives in the two-room apartment in Nusle, but instead of Greta Bauer, Milan has moved into the next room. They have decided not to share a bedroom.

Milan has kept his studio in the center, and Berta paints at home when she has time. Otherwise, every weekday she teaches for a few hours at the elementary school, and Kristýna comes to see her on Thursdays and Saturdays. She starts with Berta from the beginning: a combination of surfaces, materials, colors, contrasts, harmony, a rhythm of lines creating spatial compositions. Sometimes for inspiration, Berta shows her the work of her young students. The creative process is founded on the same principle as a children's game, she says. It has no rules, but it does have an internal logic. Rules, which mimic this logic, are usually designated from the outside, and if they must be observed, they kill the game. A game fettered with rules is merely dead repetition unless the rules themselves become something to be played with.

The creative process is incomprehensible and, from the point of view of so-called adults, just as useless and superfluous as a game. Adults do not play, and if they do, they hide it behind various purposes. They cannot admit that something is simply done for its own sake. They cannot stand any sort of capriciousness and inutility. That's why the world of adults is so terribly poor and sad!

You must always be looking; let yourself be provoked by every trifle. See and enjoy things the way they really are, as marvelous and extraordinary, and do not reduce them. Watch little children, what they find interesting. Do you think they want to bake a cake on the sand? They don't care about cakes.

They want to swim in the sand, pour it on their heads, take off their shoes and walk on it in their bare feet, or pick through it grain by grain. They want everything imaginable, just not baking cakes, which is something you have to force them to do through repetition. Be patient; watch how they can play with stones, leaves, a key or a pencil. It's mesmerizing! But you cannot imitate their freedom; you must rediscover your own within yourself, the freedom you had as a child but which they deprived you of through violence.

Berta most likes taking walks along the river, across levees, bridges, and islands. The gulls flying above the Moldau create the illusion of being near the sea and the open, distant horizon. Here, Prague is not small and cramped; one can breathe freely. Toward evening, the surface of the water is festively silvered, the lamps lit up; well-dressed people are hurrying to the theater or the Žofín Palace. Trams jangle, and a cool wind blows from the wooded slopes of Petřín Hill. For a moment, the dark stone of the castle retains its reddish tinge, then the west turns yellow, green, then pales, and the first star appears overhead.

On almost every one of her walks in the city center, she meets an acquaintance who tells her of other acquaintances also fleeing from the Nazis. Thus she accidentally learns that Max, too, is preparing to go into exile. Apparently, he's gotten a divorce and remarried. His young wife is expecting a child.

No piece of news is as painful as this one.

The Immortal One and her poet are in America. Robert Meinlich is supposedly in Paris, where the main support center of the Spanish Republicans abroad is located. From there, volunteers are being transferred across the Pyrenees to Spain. He's getting ready to fight, but Berta cannot imagine the shortsighted Meinlich with a gun in his hand. Perhaps he'll be useful in some other way.

She hears about people who have succumbed to depression and suicidal thoughts because of everything they had to leave behind and about those who, on the other hand, have grown younger and are almost mischievously hurling themselves into the unknown. They fall in love, break up, create scandals. Especially in the evening by the river, when Prague opens up alluringly before her, Berta has the feeling that the crowd of fugitives is staggering along to their own half-crazed rhythm.

For most of them, Prague is merely a way station on the path to obtaining a visa to the West, to England or America, or to the east, Palestine. Unlike the Czechoslovaks, they view the future of the country skeptically. That wound in the German flank, which according to Hitler should never have happened in the first place, does not have much hope of being saved.

Berta detaches herself from the railing and heads to the Café Slavia, to its warm and lighted windows in the autumn dusk.

Meeting in the Café Slavia

Professor!

Another specter from her past whose arrival in Prague she knew nothing about. Professor Kurz, alone at a table for two, lost in thought, doesn't hear her. She has to address him several times.

Of course he doesn't recognize her. There were so many of them in Semmering, all of them so young and garrulous, that he was unable to distinguish them. He doesn't remember her but nevertheless invites her to join him.

He asks her what she's doing in Prague, how she came to reside here, and whether she knows of any work for him. His savings are quickly running out and he will have to start looking for something. He assumes he could teach the history of philosophy or German and French. Least of all would he like to end up as a traveling salesman. He's noticed that Prague is full of German Jews going door-to-door, offering some sort of junk or other. He would rather avoid that humiliation.

Berta offers to introduce him to some immigrants with contacts. They might find something for him.

No, don't introduce me to anyone, the professor says, waving his hand. I'm here illegally. Barely do I escape the Viennese rabble, and you want to introduce me to them again? And deprive me of the only pleasant thing about emigration? No thank you.

She promises to ask around herself.

Professor Kurz looks the same as he did eighteen years ago. He must be over sixty, but his hair is almost entirely black. Anger most likely preserves.

You have no idea how the Nazis are blustering in Austria and how many people have joined them. If Hitler invades here—and that will be before you know it—they will welcome him. You'll see. I could no longer listen to those idiots swearing by Austria and condemning people according to how purely German they were. Jingoistic nationalism of any kind has always gotten on my nerves. Just like polishing the pews in church. And the combination of nationalistic zealotry and religion is so repulsive, I can't even explain it. To think that I am this or that just because I'm an Austrian or a Jew or a Czech, and furthermore, in this darkening of the mind, to assume that some god blesses me for it! Doesn't God have anything better to do? When idiots have nothing else to brandish, they resort to the nation.

The new Romans! Hah! Sniveling Romans in riding breeches!

Romans who burn books! And that idiot Spengler welcomes the advent of Roman severity. What severity? I ask you. Loutishness, brutality, violence, hatred, envy, stupidity, paranoid megalomania, and cruelty! The most repulsive things in man. And these scum call themselves Romans! As to the rest, this entire political situation is the spawn of a few syphilitics in the manic phase. Spengler—an advanced stage of mental paralysis!

Professor Kurz falls silent. Then he lifts his head. He realizes he's not here alone. So, my dear young miss or missus, from our Semmering, from the motherly embrace of Mrs. Meyer, may she rest in peace, we've found ourselves in a pretty pickle. On one side the maniac Hitler, and on the other Stalin. The exit routes are severely limited, especially for a man of my age. What country today has any use for philosophers? Palestine least of all. Eretz, as the Zionists say. My land and your land.

Professor Kurz smiles. But you know I'd go even there. Just to escape this place. I would quite gladly go to the desert and live among Arabs. Besides, I value Arab culture very much. Who other than the Arabs saved Plato and Aristotle from the religion of blinded Europeans?

I'm a Jew, but I'm old. I can't write religio-nationalist treatises in Hebrew, and the only thing more loathsome to me than working in a field is the rifle. In Palestine they're giving priority to the young, the nationalistically aware, the stupid, and the strong. From the perspective of controlled immigration, I'm completely useless. I would only take up the space of someone who could be more useful to Eretz.

No, my dear. Not even in the Promised Land, especially there, am I wanted. And I haven't yet written anything about that Judaism of theirs! But I will, I will! And you know what I'm going to call it? *The Herd Under the Sign of the Three-Headed Sleigh: Tolstoy, Marx, and Buber.* Ugh!

And what about you? Are you going to stay here and wait for Hitler?

I've gotten married here, replies Berta. According to Czechoslovak law, I'm now a Czech.

Germany also had a few laws, replies the professor. Even our Austria, fairly recently, as far as I recall. So what.

Here the situation is different, says Berta, trying to persuade him. Czechoslovakia will defend herself; I'm sure of it. The fascists have only weak support here. And there are international agreements, alliances with France, the Soviet Union.

Especially with them, the professor said with a cackle. I definitely would not rely on Stalin. And France. Don't you see whose side they're on in Spain? Are they supporting the democrats? The government that won the free elections? Far from it, my dear. France supports the fascists! And the same goes for England. To dispose of the Communists, they'd make a deal with the devil.

Did Mrs. Meyer die? asks Berta softly. The last time I saw her was at Maja's and Rudi's funeral. I kept telling myself I had to go see her, but I never mustered up the courage. All this time.

I haven't heard much about it, the man replies after a long pause. I wasn't at her funeral, either. I know only that she died a few years ago in some institution for the mentally ill in the countryside. An apparent suicide. Her husband's family covered up the whole thing. I don't even know where she's buried.

The professor waves furiously at the waiter. I just hope he doesn't ask me again if I drink coffee black or with milk. What do these Czechs have in their heads?

Mrs. Meyer is dead, Berta repeats to herself when she leaves the café. The light of the streetlamps dissolves in the light drizzle; the pavement is wet, strewn with fallen leaves. Mrs. Meyer, who sought nothing but beauty, is dead. Berta is back in the Meyers' villa. Irena sits at the piano in the empty salon and accompanies herself as she sings in her husky alto:

Oft denk' ich, sie sind nur ausgegangen!
Bald werden sie wieder nach Hause gelangen!
Der Tag ist schön! O sei nicht bang!
Sie machen nur einen weiten Gang!

Jawohl, sie sind nur ausgegangen
Und werden jetzt nach Hause gelangen.
O sei nicht bang, der Tag ist schön!
Sie machen nur den Gang zu jenen Höh'n!

Sie sind uns nur vorausgegangen
Und werden nicht wieder nach Haus verlangen!
Wir holen sie ein auf jenen Höh'n
Im Sonnenschein!
Der Tag ist schön auf jenen Höh'n![3]

CHAPTER 9

Kristýna's Confession

I HAVE TO TELL YOU THE WHOLE STORY, begins Kristýna, so you'll see how I feel. You are too young to understand. You experienced neither the war nor communism.

I remember communism quite well, objects Father Dominik. I was seventeen when it crumbled.

Oh, sorry. Kristýna smiles.

She's prepared herself a little for today and does not intend to get too upset; she'll simply tell Father Dominik what's bothering her and let him deal with it as he sees fit.

Fortunately, her fellow patients take no notice of their muffled conversation. Their eyes are fixed on the screen of a small color television set broadcasting their favorite series. From the very beginning, they have put Kristýna down as an odd character. She's always reading something while they knit and watch television. She's taciturn and in all likelihood conceited. A typical intellectual, one of them summed her up. Now nothing can surprise them, not even her whispering together with a priest.

Perhaps I'll begin, says Kristýna, with the year I was awarded a scholarship to go to France—1933. I was nineteen years old and had just graduated from high school. I was to study French there, but that was just a pretext. I actually wanted to make my way to Paris, find an art teacher, and, when my scholarship ran out, work so I could study painting. Nothing else interested me. For us at that time, *Paris* was a magic word. Anyone who wanted to achieve anything in art had to go there. I had no idea my parents would stand in my way; they never tried to restrain me in anything. But now all of a sudden Father said, firmly and severely, that I was not going anywhere. He offered several excuses—politics, Hitler, the world financial crisis—but I knew he didn't want to let me go just because I was a girl, and had I been a boy, he would have sent me on my way. I was terribly hurt. I made a huge commotion and threatened to kill myself or run away, and said that they would never see me again. Father offered me private French lessons, or I could study at the Fine Arts Academy or the Academy of Applied Arts. We could even take a trip to Paris together. But he would not concede the main point. So I began to gad about to get back at them. I fell in with a crowd and concerned myself only with boys and frippery. If I couldn't be a painter, I wouldn't be anything. Just let them see what they'd done to me.

My parents were desperate. Finally, my father came up with the idea of paying for relatively expensive lessons with the painter K. I don't know if you've heard of him; the semi-nary probably didn't offer art history. At the time, K. was quite renowned, primarily in the German-speaking world. Of course he also had a regular name, but sometime in 1912 he started to call himself K., and it stuck. He also signed his paintings with a large letter *K*. At the beginning of the thirties, he moved from Vienna to Prague and even painted President Masaryk's portrait. My father was a respected architect and moved about in high society, where he met the artist. K. invited my father to his studio on the embankment, and without my knowledge my father took some of my work to show him. K. confirmed that

I had talent and agreed to tutor me. Most likely, he needed the money; at that time poverty was ubiquitous.

Father correctly surmised that I would not refuse such a teacher. I started going to see him regularly and cooled off for a bit. I should tell you I was quite attractive at that time. And terribly vain. I believed there was not a man alive who did not desire me, and I left no one in peace, not even the painter K., even though he was much older. We began something and things started getting complicated; our student-teacher relationship began to deteriorate. Nevertheless, K. was a fabulous teacher. He supported me and gave me the courage to paint. My parents saw the results and were pleased. Of course, they had no idea I was also sleeping with him

At the time, I was more concerned with being admired than with art. I was particularly proud of my body, my hair; I admired my eyes and eyebrows and lips. I could not get enough of my beauty and required a lover who would appreciate me. This was probably because as a little girl I was ugly; I really was. I got over it around the age of sixteen. My beauty and the power I had over men were as new and exhilarating as a drug. I had lots of admirers, and K. began to grow jealous. He wanted me all to himself and insisted that I come see him more often and become his assistant. Thereby he hoped to bind me to him. I knew that if I complied, my painting would go to hell; I would be completely devoured. Surreptitiously, I began attending evening drawing courses at the Academy of Arts. At the same time, I pretended everything was fine and even promised I would consider his offer. And I went on sleeping with him, not because I was especially attracted to him, but because he was a famous artist. I was a coward. I entangled myself in lies until I no longer knew who I was. It was a really strange time. Until

I met Berta. It was she who induced me to take an interest in things other than myself.

At that time, a lot of people frequented the studio on the embankment, because it was a sort of center for the German resistance abroad. I met a good many real celebrities, as they say today, and the enamored K. showed me off and introduced me to everyone, so that I felt terribly important. Berta came with a group of fresh émigrés. At first glance, she seemed an unassuming and inconspicuous woman, no longer young. She was wearing a three-quarter-length dark brown corduroy skirt, a jacket of the same color, and an apricot orange blouse. I can still see her today. She had a large leather purse over her shoulder. I was complaining to her that my father had forbidden me to go to Paris. She praised the sketch I had begun, told me she had taught for a long time in Vienna, but mostly young children, and said that K. was an excellent and original teacher. She had admired him since childhood and had seen him teach at the academy in Dresden, which she had once visited with friends. At the time, she was still living in Berlin. His way of behaving with the students had left a deep impression on her and later she often tried to imitate it.

K. was surprised. He didn't remember any visit in Dresden.

If she had been prettier, he definitely would have remembered, joked Berta.

It's true, she wasn't very pretty, but I was immediately captivated by her eyes. When she looked at you, it was as if some kind of light were bursting forth, or something like that. I don't really know how to explain it. It was like being engulfed in light and warmth.

At this time, she had exactly ten years to live.

She was on the last transport the Germans dispatched from Terezín to Auschwitz on the twenty-eighth of October, 1944.

Nobody survived. But even if the entire transport had not been going to the gas chambers, she wouldn't have made it alive. She would have definitely ended up with at least two children; they were always hanging on her. And all women carrying or accompanied by children automatically went to their deaths. When I read about it long after the war, I suddenly saw clearly how Berta died. She was calming and comforting someone else's children until they suffocated.

After a while, I became friends with Berta. By then, she was already married to an acquaintance of mine, Milan Drůza. I started going to see them and broke off my relationship with the painter K. With a single blow, I rent that entire web of lies. No longer could I learn anything from him, but in Berta I sensed something profoundly intriguing. I didn't know what it was, but I set off after the scent like an animal. Now I know what it was that attracted me. When we met, Berta was going through a difficult and complicated period; later she told me she was becoming reconciled with herself and her losses. Her entire being was permeated with a kind of ease; she played at nothing and pretended nothing. The absence of fear in her reflections allowed her to see extraordinarily sharply. She was almost cruel in her simplicity, and people around her were not always willing to view things so clearly and directly. When I was with Berta, I knew I was on the right path and could not go astray. Everything false melted away before her presence, and I could rely on her internal compass. Until I was able to go my own way. That's what I wanted to learn: how to go my own way. How to plow through all the rubbish I carried around with me and get through to the pure, absolute source. Then I would be able to paint well. Of this I was certain.

Truthfulness, it is possible to get across truthfulness. To a certain extent.

At the time, I was studying at the Academy of Applied Arts, but I was unable to finish because the Nazis closed it. But I'm jumping ahead. After March of '38, when Hitler marched into Vienna, we could not stop crying. The mobilization, Munich, demobilization, the influx of refugees from border regions . . . Berta took Munich terribly hard; she identified with the Czechs in every respect. She took it harder even than the occupation of Austria. When Milan returned from his company on September thirtieth, angry and disgruntled because he had wanted to fight but was not allowed, Berta said, It is the end of Czechoslovakia. Remember it as it is now. We were sitting around a table in Nusle, listening to the radio. President Beneš was speaking in a squeaky voice, and Berta foretold a hasty end. Without allies, we haven't a chance, she said.

Beneš abdicated on the fifth of October and went into exile. Anyone who was able fled to the West—as did the painter K.—and Berta feared Hitler would invade at any time and that no one would be able to go anywhere. Surprisingly, she didn't consider another emigration. She only wanted to leave the city, which seemed to her like a trap. In January 1939, her old friend Meinlich got her a visa to Palestine. But she would have to leave immediately and alone. Once she got there, it would be possible to get a visa for Milan, but this was not for certain, and Berta vowed not to go anywhere without her husband. The same thing happened six months later when Max Jauner, who had managed to get out of Vienna in time, invited her to England. The pretext for the government offices was an exhibition of her and Jauner's designs from the time they worked together. Anyone else would have given anything for such a chance, but Berta refused to leave. At the time, we almost got into a fight over it. I was tremendously afraid for her. Transports from the Protectorate had not yet begun, but the first regulations concerning Jews had been promulgated. It was clear where things were headed, and that Czech citizenship would not protect anyone from the misery that lay ahead. Also, daily existence was becoming more and more uncertain. It was only a matter of time before Berta would be fired from the textile factory—where she and Milan designed fabric for fifty crowns a week—and turned out of their apartment, which they had just managed to furnish. Nevertheless, she would not go anywhere. I am certain that I have nothing to gain by leaving, she said to me, but I do have something to lose.

By then, they had already moved to Hronov, near Náchod, on the Polish border. They had chosen Náchod because part of Milan's family had come from there; thus they would at least have some acquaintances around. Furthermore, the textile shops there were hiring workers to replace the Germans who had decided to move to the Reich capital.

Insofar as it was possible, I would go for a weekend visit at least once a month, even though it was awfully far. Mostly, I would take them cigarettes, which were rationed and not meant for Jews.

I also took them coffee and tea, fruit, when it was available; it depended on what I could lay my hands on. They felt neither abandoned nor unhappy in the countryside. Berta was fond of Hronov, she said, primarily because she could breathe freely there. It was not a typical small town, crammed in around a square. Hronov took up an entire shallow valley, and little villas dotted the surrounding hills. When you looked down at it, you saw more spaces than houses. Just behind the Drůzas' home—a yellow two-story apartment building across from the train station—the forest began, and in the center of the town, along the Metuje River, stretched a park with a bathing area and marvelous trees that had been there since the invasion of the Swedes during the Thirty Years' War.

In this region, textile producers were called rag-and-bone men, and the town boasted plenty of them, several large families. Instead of cottages, they built little villas with glassed-in verandas, and in the twenties and thirties they turned Náchod and Hronov into cultural municipalities. Hronov had a beautiful new theater and exhibition hall, where Berta, despite all the public notices and anti-Semitic limitations, had an exhibition as late as 1941.

It was a curious region. The locals said that the ground there was still suffused with the blood of soldiers from the Austro-Prussian War. One theory—and there was more than one—suggested that after the Battle at White Mountain, in 1620, a good many Czech Brethren took up shelter there. In secret, beneath the cover of official Catholicism, they managed to preserve their religion during the entire time of the Hapsburg persecution. The Protestant liturgy was passed down from generation to generation and, along with it, some sort of hidden memory, a sense of continuity and pride in Czech history. Apparently, from this very germ emerged the famous National Revivalists. I don't know. I really liked it there.

There were several graphic artists living in Hronov and Náchod; professors and students had returned from the universities, which were being closed. Milan was a convivial, outgoing person; he played the accordion, liked his drink, and was always inviting people over. I often asked myself if Berta wasn't bothered by all this, but she seemed game. When the Germans banned Jews from pubs and cafés, naturally her husband had to turn their home into a café.

At the end of August 1940, when the first German bombs were being dropped on London, Berta discovered she was pregnant. Three months had gone by, and everything seemed to be in order. She had even started to show. It was simply a miracle.

Berta confided in me that the Lord had undoubtedly rewarded her for not leaving for England. She was forgiven. I had no idea why she should be forgiven. For what? She never talked much about her past with me, and I didn't know that Jauner had been her lover. But when she started in with God, I was quite surprised. I had always seen her as an atheist. She also said the child would be named Paul or Paula, after the painter Paul Klee, who had passed away that year in Switzerland. She mourned him as if he had been a relative, even though they had never been on intimate terms. She had studied under him in Weimar and said that her child could be him. Did she also believe in reincarnation? Pregnant women say all sorts of things, I guess.

I've told you already that when I met Berta, she was living in a state of almost brutal truthfulness. Now all of this changed. She was enraptured, carried away by her own imagination. With every visit, I found her somewhat younger and more disheveled. It was touching but at the same time did not jibe with everything going on around us. The Germans were announcing victory after victory and progressing more quickly than even they had expected, conquering one territory after another. More absurd and malicious anti-Jewish edicts were being issued, which had no other end than raising doubts as to whether the Jews were human beings at all—both among the Jews themselves and those around them. Every week there was something new, along with disgusting, seditious newspaper articles.

And it was in this atmosphere that Berta happily awaited the birth of the child she'd always longed for, a Jew.

Milan and I were infected by Berta's enthusiasm. We consoled ourselves with the thought that they were safe in Hronov and everything would be all right, that nothing worse could befall them. Sooner or later, Hitler would lose, and peace would ensue. I banished my gloomy thoughts and concentrated on getting more fruit for Berta, which she needed now.

Then came winter and Christmas. I went to see Berta and Milan immediately after the Feast of Saint Stephen and was supposed to stay almost ten days. Berta and I had really been looking forward to this holiday. Finally we would have more than just a Saturday and part of Sunday for ourselves. In Prague, I went to work—I was working in a factory producing caps and hats—but I was given a vacation until January sixth. I spent Christmas Eve with my family and then left for Hronov.

On New Year's Eve, Milan's friends invited us to a cottage in the hills not far from Náchod. I think the place was called Hell, and to get there we had to climb up from the valley by foot. In view of Berta's condition, we argued about whether we should go, but in the end Berta herself insisted we go. The mountain air, she said, would do her good, and a little walk wouldn't hurt.

We set out from Hronov immediately after lunch, but when we started to climb the hill, it was already getting dark and the stars were coming out. Milan, loaded down with sleeping bags, clothing, and three days' worth of food, quickly took the lead. It was one of the most beautiful moments that Berta and I ever experienced together. We stopped often so she could rest, and we gazed up at the stars and inhaled the fresh air, redolent with the scent of snow and pine needles. The child Berta was carrying inside her invigorated and filled us both with joy. The war had vanished, our anxieties melted away, and everything was pointing to the future: blessed, sweet, and miraculous. After a while, we arrived at the cottage. Our friends were already awaiting us with hot punch, the cabin was heated, and food was ready. Usually I'm somewhat sad on New Year's Eve. I don't see any reason for celebration. Thinking about the future frightens me. Maybe everyone feels that way and that's why they drink and shoot off fireworks, to drown it out. But New Year's Eve in 1940 was beautiful. We were happy to be together and grateful for every pleasant moment, since those times were rare. We were warm, we had something to eat and drink, and we could sing and dance. Suddenly, we saw everything as a precious gift. The war was good for that. One experienced everything more intensely, especially love and friendship.

The next morning, we awoke to a beautiful day; the sun was shining and all around the cottage the snow sparkled. Some went skiing, while Berta and I sunbathed in front of the cottage and cooked. Unlike me, Berta loved to cook. And she knew how. She could conjure up a good meal from almost nothing— a few potatoes and a couple of cloves of garlic, for example. She didn't consider cooking degrading, nor did she see it as a waste of time. Not even cleaning and other housework bothered her. And she was quite skillful at it. We spent three days in the mountains, each more beautiful than the last, and on January fourth we descended into the valley and returned to Hronov by the local train. Berta and Milan had to go back to work, but I still had two days of vacation left.

On the fifth, Berta came home from work early; her belly was aching. She claimed it was nothing but went to lie down just in case. Toward evening, she started to bleed a little. Milan called the doctor, who wanted to take her to the hospital immediately. The maternity ward was in Náchod, and Milan went with them. There was no room in the car for me.

I waited at home. Even though I didn't believe in God, I prayed. I kept reliving that feeling of supernatural happiness that Berta and I had experienced just a few days earlier. Was it possible that this feeling had been a deception?

I waited until around one o'clock; outside it had started to snow. Then I heard the doctor's car driving up to the house, followed by footsteps on the stairs. It was Milan; he had come back alone. Berta was still in the hospital. They had given her some medicine to keep her calm, and she had to remain in bed. In a couple of days, however, she would be well. We were both exhausted and went straight to bed.

It was snowing heavily when we woke up in the morning. Milan set out for the train station but soon came back, saying the trains were not running and he wasn't going to the factory because he had been called by the municipality to go and clear snow. He asked me to go to the post office and call the hospital. It took a long time to battle my way through the drifts, and even longer before I was put through. There was probably a line down because of the snow. When I finally got through to the hospital, I was told that Mrs. Drůzová was sleeping and everything was fine. But we had to say good-bye to the baby.

Why? It was as if I had gone dumb.

The doctor was impatient; she didn't want to waste time with me. Mrs. Drůzová gave birth during the night, but the baby was dead, she told me. It was only in its fifth month and wouldn't have survived anyway. Let us be glad that Mrs. Drů-zová survived. You can come pick her up tomorrow.

She hung up.

The trains were not running; the roads were bogged down with snow, and there was no way to get to Náchod unless I went on skis. It was only eight kilometers and I knew the way, but in this snowstorm you couldn't see a foot in front of you. I considered it nevertheless. I felt dreadful when I imagined Berta all alone. But in the end, I was glad just to make it those few blocks home from the post office. Milan came home a little after I did; it was already getting dark. They had refused to release him from his snow-removal work any earlier. He always looked healthy, and this evening he was simply radiant. His face was red, and he was happy, as if he'd been drinking. But he hadn't. It was simply from working in the fresh air all day. Milan loved outdoor physical labor and couldn't stand the unventilated and badly lit textile factory. He had not the slightest suspicion that there might have been anything wrong with Berta and the baby; the doctor had promised that everything would turn out all right, and Milan trusted people. Thus the blow was all the heavier. And he had to hear it from me, of all people. I started crying, but not Milan. He went completely white and clenched his jaw, so that his cheeks bulged. Then he got up and left the room. He shuffled about and came back with an unopened bottle of brandy, placed two glasses on the table, and opened the bottle. His hands were trembling, and when he began pouring, a little of the clear liquid splashed onto Berta's green tablecloth.

We sat and drank, both of us submerged in our own thoughts. At one point, Milan placed his hands on the table, palms up, and bowed his head between them. It was such an expression of helplessness, those up-turned palms, as if he no longer sought to resist anything. I lay my hand on his, palm-to-palm. His was much bigger than mine, dry, somewhat coarse, and warm.

He started to sob, his forehead on the table. Have you ever noticed that men don't know how to cry? A man's weeping always sounds awkward and crude, as if it's forcing its way out. As if crying hurts them physically.

All at once, he knelt down and embraced me, his hands around my waist, and spewed out everything he was afraid of: that Berta would never be happy with him, that Hitler would win the war, that all of the Jews would be taken away and slaughtered.

Then we made love. On the floor of Berta's kitchen.

Kristýna closes her eyes. Presses her eyelids firmly shut. No, no, she is not going to cry.

My lap was hot and wet from his tears. I begged him not to do this and at the same time spread my legs. Then I was no longer pleading, because his tongue was in my mouth; but my pleasure increased and I started to scream. Never had I heard myself shout like this before, in a completely unfamiliar voice. I splayed out beneath him and held on, washed over with hot fluid and sweat until, at the peak of one of the waves, I was gathered up by another, higher one, which turned me inside out and consumed me in a long, drawn-out spasm.

When I opened my eyes again, the first thing I saw was a lamp with a blue paper lampshade. The lamp, veiled according to wartime regulations, brought me back to reality.

Milan rolled over on his back, one arm draped over his eyes. He didn't move. I got up and locked myself in the bathroom. First I washed. Then I sat down on the bidet and tried to gather at least a few of my thoughts. What should I do now? I wondered. I wanted to pack up my things quickly and leave that very night. I didn't want to say anything to Milan or even see him. And the next day, Berta was coming home! I must leave right now! I thought. I got up, then sat down again. It was dark outside and still snowing heavily. Not even the streetlights were working. The trains were not running, and the train station was closed. To set out on skis would have been suicidal.

I listened for sounds in the apartment. Besides the ticking of the clock, I heard absolutely nothing, not even a whisper. I opened the door and left the bathroom on tiptoe. Milan was asleep on the floor. He lay on his belly, with his arms spread wide and his torso twisted, as if he were throwing something, getting rid of something. Then I knew what he reminded me of: a javelin thrower from antiquity. A beautiful statue of a Greek youth, the kind we had studied in school. I brought over a blanket and covered him up. Then I changed into my nightshirt and crawled into bed. Sitting beneath the covers with my knees pulled up beneath my chin, I thought of Berta. I hoped she had been given some pills, was sleeping and not in pain.

It stopped snowing at daybreak, says Kristýna, continuing her confession.

Father Dominik is sitting by the bed, his head inclined toward her mouth, as if he is praying. Kristýna is propped up on two pillows. Her leg is aching much more now. It hurts so much that at times she has to interrupt her story and wait for the shooting pain to subside. The doctors have already established the date of the operation; she has to hold out two more days. Two more days. If they hadn't promised the pain would cease, or decrease markedly, she would not want to go on. If she thought it would continue for a month, let's say, she would leap from the window.

Sometimes she asks the nurse for a painkiller, but she doesn't dare ask too often. Beneath the nurse's severe gaze, she feels like a fraud.

It stopped snowing, repeats Kristýna. I got up and quickly packed my backpack. I didn't have much; I had put on most of the clothing I had brought with me—stockings, pants, two sweaters, a coat. I peered into the kitchen; Milan was still sleeping, curled up beneath the blanket. I tore a piece of paper from my sketchbook and scribbled him a note, asking him to tell Berta that I had to go back to Prague, for otherwise I would be fired. I would come as soon as possible and I was thinking of her. About what had happened between us—nothing. I could come up with only platitudes and clichés, and after a moment I decided it would be better to initiate a bilateral silence right now. Lay it to rest without comment. I was sure Milan would understand my intention and would certainly not want to hurt Berta. I placed the letter next to his head and crept outside. I took my skis from the hallway and set out along the snow-covered road in the direction of Náchod. I was hoping there wouldn't be as much snow there and that from Náchod I would somehow be able to make it to Hradec Králové and from there to Prague.

It was a calm, clear morning. The sun had just come up and the snow glistened all around, soft and undisturbed.

My conscience troubled me, but at the same time I could not suppress a feeling of exhilaration as I moved through the snow. At times, I forgot about Berta and felt like singing.

It was the end of February when I finally got the courage to go back to Hronov again. I remember it quite well; the first snowdrops were being sold in the streets of Prague.

The snow was beginning to melt in the foothills. Berta and I went on long walks and listened to the springlets flowing from the fields beneath the crust of frozen snow. I don't know if you've ever had the opportunity to hear anything like that. Each springlet sounds completely different; it's marvelous. Berta could listen for hours. She said each springlet had its own story, often quite amusing.

She kept dashing outside, in every kind of weather. Over and over, she would walk around the hills surrounding Hronov, and in her coat pockets she carried her cigarettes, a small sketch-book, and a pencil. Her dog would trot alongside beside her, a fox terrier she had found somewhere on the streets.

She was different now. Her previous ease had become indifference. One could see that in the depths of her soul she couldn't care less about Hitler and the entire war, even about the future of the Jews or any future whatsoever. She had sealed herself off and modestly withdrawn, trying not to hurt anyone.

In the spring, she was fired from the factory and had to live on Milan's pay. Berta sewed a little at home, producing coverlets and pillows, but usually there was nothing to make them from and nobody to make them for. Milan managed to hold on to his job primarily because of the family of his non-Jewish father in Hronov. Because of them, they had something to eat and Berta something to smoke, which was most important for her.

She drew and painted almost nonstop. There was also a shortage of paper and paints, and oils were completely unavailable; occasionally you could get some watercolors and chalk. But Berta painted with anything she could get her hands on and on any kind of surface—without thinking and without any apparent intent. Often she would select only a wedge of a certain object: the pleat of a curtain, part of her hand, a portion of a tree, Milan's back as he washed up.

During her next phase, she drew even closer to the objects and began to study their structure. She would draw them as something like ornaments, corresponding to one another. It was so interesting. In her pictures, she abolished geometric space. She divested objects of their volume and weight; they were no longer separated from one another.

In the summer and fall, she painted primarily flowers: the light permeating the petals, the feathering of the leaflets, the arrangement of the stems in water. Her bouquets from 1941 are breathtaking, and the most beautiful one, the begonias, I have at home.

As far as these final paintings go, I should admit that I was jealous. I could never paint something so immediate, so light, so luminous and beautiful. It was in these, I think, that Berta's artistic personality fully manifested itself for the first time.

Sometime in the middle of September, an edict was issued, stating that Jews must display a star on the front left side of their coats and they could not stray from their dwelling places. The first transports from Prague began in October. In November, Berta and Milan were informed that they had to move out of their apartment. It was by no means a beautiful apartment, but someone had taken a liking to it. After a long search, they managed to find two attic rooms in a small villa just above the Sokol organization's gym. It had a marvelous view of the entire Hronov valley, and Berta, despite their penury, managed to fix it up so that it did not come across as depressing in the least. I was able to visit them only two more times. My family kicked up an enormous fuss. Associating with Jews really was dangerous, or at least that's what everyone thought. My father started having heart trouble and used that to blackmail me.

I keep talking about Berta and avoiding my relationship with her husband. It's not easy to admit. At first Milan and I tried to pretend that nothing had happened between us, but we couldn't keep it up. During my visit at the end of February, we had become lovers.

Milan claimed Berta was shunning him. He said she had always remained aloof, and now they had grown completely estranged in the physical sense. If he had any remorse, he didn't tell me about it.

I fell in love with him. We slept together only a few more times; it wasn't a genuine relationship, because we simply did not have the opportunity. There was something desperate in the way we discharged our mutual desire. Everything around us was abnormal; we couldn't hope for anything. For the three of us, no future existed. Berta found her escape in drawing, and Milan and I in moments of passion, which were possible to mistake for happiness.

We were an odd trio. It was not only the two of us who lied. I am certain that Berta, too, just out of consideration, tried to pretend that living with Milan was still important to her.

The last time I saw Berta was just before their deportation to Terezín in the spring of 1942. I went to help her and Milan pack up the fifty kilos of luggage they were allowed. I never would have guessed how little this was. Again and again, we had to unpack the suitcases and backpacks and go through everything that, on closer inspection, was not absolutely necessary. We would discard a few things, pack it all up, and weigh the suitcases again, and when it was still not enough, we took everything out again. Checklists drawn up by those who had already departed for Terezín were being issued at the Jewish town hall. They listed the items most necessary for the trip, but even with this, it was not easy.

What was I thinking about while packing? I no longer know. I was probably trying to concentrate on specific tasks. Throughout the entire war, we always tried to concentrate on specific tasks: acquiring sugar, fruit, cigarettes; filling out forms; getting home from work. We exhausted ourselves with our day-to-day duties, and the Germans always made sure there were plenty of them. So there was neither the time nor the strength to see the big picture and pose specific questions: Where were they taking them? What would become of them? Why didn't any of us stand up for them? Why?

So I helped them pack their bags. This was the extent of my devotion to the two people closest to me on Earth, those whom some primitive, evil, absurd power had set out to take from me. My personal contribution lay in packing suitcases. All my courage had been spent on defying my parents and going to Hronov to pack!

When we finally finished, we went to bed. Berta and I in one room and Milan in the other. I didn't even have the chance to embrace him one last time. I lay wide-awake, longing to make love to him, to say good-bye the only way possible for the two of us. I waited for Berta to fall asleep, but she didn't. She lay beside me, sobbing till dawn.

I didn't even move and pretended to be asleep. I was yearning for her husband, and Berta was in the way. At the final moment of our friendship, the only time I could have ever been of use to her, she stood in my way. With everything she meant to me and everything she had done for me. That is the horrible truth.

I was not allowed to accompany them all the way to the train; that would have seemed too much like a normal departure. I returned to Prague in the afternoon with Berta's diaries, a few of her pictures, and a packet of books she didn't want to leave in the care of her Hronov aunts.

Only several years after the war did I decide to look at her diaries. The last entry was dated two days before they left for Terezín, and when I read it, I understood why Berta had been crying that final night. She wasn't afraid of leaving, it was something much worse. She had the feeling she had utterly wasted her life. And I could have proved to her that she was wrong. I could have reminded her of all those children she had taught, everything she had given Milan and me, what she had sacrificed for people she barely knew, in Vienna and in Spain. I could have talked about her marvelous final paintings.

But I didn't.

"So, we are heading to the end," she wrote. "I accomplished nothing as an artist, and as a woman I failed utterly. This is the balance of almost forty-two years. Desperately do I regret losing this wasted life of mine. Even more than if I had managed to fulfill it."

Are you listening to me?

The young man leaning over the bed nods.

Surely you will tell me I should not blame myself for Berta's death. Why blame oneself? Why not sleep, even after fifty years? Why harbor such animosity toward oneself? Could I have changed anything? Everyone acknowledges that I couldn't have. If we leave out the fact that I could have gone to my death with her.

That wouldn't have helped anyone, the priest says, finally breaking his silence.

Do you really think so! After all, they couldn't slaughter all the Jews along with their non-Jewish friends, neighbors, and acquaintances. Not even the Germans would manage to do that!

Kristýna falls silent. Then after a moment, she says, Perhaps you've seen pictures of children in Terezín. They're fairly well known.

The priest nods. He dimly recalls going with his parents to the Jewish museum once when he was little and seeing some children's drawings—mostly of butterflies.

Those were by Berta's pupils. Survivors claim that only thanks to her did they remain children at least a little bit in the concentration camp. They did not grow stupefied; they did not get lost in the chaos, the absurdity, the sorrow. Berta gave them a reprieve from their everyday fears, although they might be damaged by such fear, they would not be destroyed by it. The children worshiped her. She was fun, full of energy and ideas. They say she seemed happy.

Outside the hospital, it is dark but it's not late yet, barely five o'clock. Tiny drops of rain or wet snow cling to the windowpanes, glistening, and the wind leads them in a dance across the smooth glass.

And you believe that? asks the priest.

That she saved them?

That she was happy.

Yes, replies Kristýna. I, too, didn't believe it at first. I thought they were lying to me so I wouldn't feel so sorry for Berta. But then I thought about it, for a long time, almost fifty years, and now I am certain. In Terezín, Berta relinquished herself. They had taken responsibility away from her and therewith the feeling of guilt that accompanied her everywhere. In a forcibly constricted, maximally circumscribed space, she found some sort of peace. She had been condemned to it, and perhaps precisely because of that, she felt safe there. Moreover, she could devote herself to the children as much as they needed her, without doubting and reproaching herself for neglecting her own work. In Terezín, the maintenance and development of sensitivity and fantasy were more important than getting enough to eat. Berta believed in salvation through art. This was the faith that had attracted her to teaching in the twenties, and she never abandoned it. In art, she sought what you seek in God. Truth.

I seek love, objects the priest.

My friend believed that the creative spirit had the ability to affect matter and transform it. That fantasy had the power to overcome what most people understand as the only binding reality—that is, the given conditions, patterns, and rules of human existence. Berta was a Communist but never a Marxist. Do you see what I mean? She did not believe it was right to displace one form of violence with another, one form of matter with another. She was convinced that a genuinely perceptive being would not be able to exploit another, nor would it allow itself to be humiliated. An internally free, sensitive, and creative being full of fantasy must have the ability to change the world by means other than force. The only revolution she served completely was the revolution of the human spirit. And human perception.

The young priest wipes his face with his handkerchief—he has scratched his pimples bloody. Should I come tomorrow?

Kristýna shakes her head. Tomorrow is the last day before the operation, she says. My family is coming to bid farewell. Of course they don't call it that. The word *farewell* may not be uttered in front of them.

How do you feel?

I'm in terrible pain. And I'm afraid. I would like to finish my confession.

Milan left for Auschwitz before Berta. He was young, useful, and he survived. We got married a year after the end of the war, in the spring of 1946, when it was clear that Berta had not survived by some miracle. In September, Mirek was born. In 1948, Milan left for Israel and never returned. I asked for a divorce in his absence, and the authorities complied. I gave up his name, and for our son, as well. Mirek grew up thinking his father had died. I didn't tell him his father was a Jew or that he had been in a concentration camp. I saw no need to burden him with it. Everything was still too recent. If he asked about his father, I would make something up. I kept postponing the truth as long as possible, waiting for the right moment, but it never came, and then it seemed pointless. It would have been such a psychological blow. And for what? Is it not better to love your idea of something than to know the truth and hate?

Why do you think he would have hated him?

The old woman remains silent.

Is your ex-husband still alive?

No, he died.

So you've had some news of him?

He wrote me for years—about himself and his new family; he asked about Mirek.

Didn't he ever want to see him?

He did. Two years before his death, Milan asked if he could come; the borders were loosening then.

And you didn't let him?

No.

Did he ever explain why he left you?

Because of the Holocaust. Because of all the people the Germans murdered. But we were alive, Mirek and I. We needed him. He hurt me terribly. I could not forgive him!

Mrs. Hladková. The young man clasps the cold, soft, brown-spotted hands plaited with dark veins. Mrs. Hladková, he repeats, comforting the sobbing woman. This is your greatest torment. Mrs. Hladková, you should try to forgive him.

He's dead anyway!

That doesn't matter.

And if I can't?

Then not even you can be forgiven.

Chapter 10

Aaron's Leap

WHEN HE OPENS THE DOOR TO THE TERRACE, he sees the desert. Since moving into his expensive new apartment in a modern building on a hill at the edge of Jerusalem, he hasn't had time to get used to the view: the stony wasteland, which changes hues according to the color of the sky.

His neighbors' terraces on both sides are submerged in greenery. Mr. Roth on the right even keeps parrots in his little jungle, which he waters regularly with an automatic sprinkler, even when he isn't there.

Aaron still has not had time to settle into his apartment properly, let alone develop his terrace. For now, it's enough that it provides shade.

Aaron's mother is proud of her son's apartment. She brags about it to her neighbors in the Arab quarter, from which she never managed to relocate. She tells everyone: Our Aaron has really come up in the world! Nevertheless, she reproaches him about his divorce every chance she gets.

It is Sunday evening and Aaron has just dropped his son off at his ex-wife's. She allowed Aaron to take him for the long weekend. They went to the sea, and he spent a lot of money without getting anywhere. He asked himself where, exactly, he was trying to get in his relationship with the eight-year-old.

Why does he always feel so dissatisfied when he returns him to his mother? He could never be to Viktor what his own father was to him, but perhaps somehow he'll be able to make up for this insufficiency. And prove he can achieve his son's love.

Just like he achieved everything else. As for himself, his parents could provide only what was necessary. They had come to Israel from Morocco forty years earlier, and both his mother and his father wore themselves down in menial and badly paid jobs. His dad worked himself to death.

Viktor must have it easier than he had, Aaron would see to that.

He takes off his clothes and steps in the shower, which still feels new. Then he shaves, puts on some cologne, and gets dressed. He likes carrying out these minor operations no matter where he is. The simple feeling of his own touch calms him, and the fragrance is soothing. When he opens the closet, he notes with satisfaction the row of shirts, coats, pants, and under-clothes ironed and folded by his Russian housekeeper, and even now the thought flashes through his mind that it's pleasant to live alone. Despite everything that's missing.

At precisely eight o'clock, he takes the elevator down to the garage, gets into his Honda, and takes off to the other side of town, where Lu lives.

He promised to take her to dinner.

Aaron's birthday is today. He's forty-four years old.

It's strange how many people there are on the street. And they don't look like they're in any hurry. On the contrary, they're loitering around or staggering about near the walls. A man inadvertently steps in his path, staring off somewhere else. He's wearing a black hat. Probably an Orthodox Jew, thinks Aaron. His dark back blocking the alleyway. How can I get him to move out of the way? Aaron is in a hurry. He says something in Hebrew, but the man doesn't understand. He slowly turns around to face Aaron, his face concealed by his hat. He doesn't have any whiskers. He's not a Jew at all, Aaron suddenly realizes. He's got a bomb beneath his black kaftan! Aaron hears his own distant cry. The thought that maybe he's asleep flashes through Aaron's mind. He shouts and at the same time reaches out his hand and waves it in front of him. His fingers meet a void. Death is dissolving. He hears a woman's voice, a woman calling to him, but he's too tired; he must sink away, sleep. He comes back.

The city is gray and black. He weaves his way to the main square, through the people loitering and standing around; the trees are spaced evenly apart, leafless. They look like a burned-out field. Aaron is pushing a cart in front of him, which makes his progress through the overcrowded city unbelievably difficult. Finally, he makes it to the gate and drags the cart across the threshold. It's not a barracks, but a belfry. He must climb to the top along the winding wooden stairs. It's not easy with the cart, but if it gets lost or stolen, he'll be shot. He keeps climbing, always taking two steps at a time, then pulls; the cart is lighter than he expected. He looks around amid the dust-covered tangles of rope and the shadows of the beams. She is here, lying on the ground, in something that looks like trampled straw. He throws up her skirt, the material is soft and abundant. Another deception, he thinks, but then his palm finds the hot, moist lap and he sinks into it without touching her anymore. The delight he takes in his groin borders on agony. In his dream, she is at his mercy and he can do whatever he wants. With this in mind, he decides to show the girl what he can do. He starts waving his arms vigorously and ascends just below the roof of the belfry. There he grabs hold of one of the ropes and swings to the other side, lets go, and seems to be rolling in the air. He is quite worthy of admiration! He is going to show the girl how to fly. He leaps from the window of the belfry and transforms his fall into a gliding flight. It's higher than he expected, but he is not afraid. He just has to maintain his height. They soar together for a moment above the city before landing on the parapets, a wide, round escarpment covered with grass. Beyond the parapets is a dike and beyond that the countryside is bathed in the soft light of the sun. It's a garden with rosy hills and blue shadows, with carefully trimmed shrubbery and the upright fingers of cypresses, arranged into several levels in a perfect harmony of colors and shapes. Everything is remarkably pliant and sharply drawn. How delightful to rest one's eyes upon it, thinks Aaron. Never before has he experienced such acuity of vision. He examines each individual shape, then turns to Milena. Her face has the same pliancy, clarity, and diversity as the countryside. Aaron watches her, takes her in. He no longer desires to touch her; he wants only to stare and stare.

Where's the cart? He forgot it in the belfry. He must go back and find the cart or they'll shoot him. Aaron descends into the blackish gray city streets, alone. Milena has disappeared. The street that previously led to the square is no longer there. He has to find another one and follow it back to the barracks, which is actually the belfry, and enter through the back door. The city is empty and it's getting dark. Venomous dogs idle about the street corners. One bite can kill a man. Is it possible that everyone died while he was on the ramparts? The deadline is approaching. Another moment and a shot will ring out. He's not going to make it.

He hears his own distant cry.

His fingers meet a void. The shadow of a woman towers over him.

Lu?

What's the matter?

I had a dream about Terezín.

They make love half-asleep, while his body still clings to the delight of the dream. He transfers it to the woman whose contours are still out of focus. She could easily be the other one.

19 April 1949, Kibbutz Givat Ada
My Dear,

If you hadn't let me go—and you did have this power over me—I would have killed myself anyway. Isn't it better, after all, that I'm alive? Even if I'm in Israel? I could not stay with you, but you must believe that I never stopped being with you and Mirek.

It's not because I'm a Jew, but because I survived. You cannot judge me! I am beyond all categories and judgments. I do not say this proudly. I survived Auschwitz. But how was I supposed to survive after Auschwitz? You did not help me at all. I could not pretend that nothing had happened, that the world was once again all right. Like you and everyone else. You were not interested in me. You just wanted me to be "normal," to adapt.

I had to go somewhere where I wouldn't be so alone with what I had lived through. And I wanted to work. Physically, from morning to night, work myself to the point of exhaustion, never stop, and mainly not to think. Each moment of hesitation could prove fatal. Dig up the desert? Fight? All the better. I longed for something to fight for! To rid myself of the feeling of humiliation. To prove that, despite everything, I was still a person.

I am not nor will I ever be "myself" again. I do not feel, I do not think the way I used to. It was not my legs I lost during the war, but a piece of my soul. At first glance it's invisible, and for that, all the worse. I would only be a hindrance and destroy both you and our son. I know you cannot understand me, but you must believe me. Please believe me!

Please kiss Mirek for me. Kiss Mirek.

Milan

The other patients have turned off the television and gone to sleep. Each snores in a different key and a different rhythm. Kristýna turns on the little lamp above her bed, and a narrow circle of light falls on her pillow, which could not possibly bother anyone. On a plastic tray on her night table lie sleeping pills and pain pills, but she doesn't want to take them. She needs a clear mind.

At home, on the lowest shelf of her bookcase, between tied-up bundles of *Art* magazine and a box of clippings, is a sealed envelope filled with letters written on paper as thin as cigarette paper. It is sealed because Kristýna no longer wanted to concern herself with the contents. She intended to weigh it down with a stone and throw it in a river or stream at the first opportunity, which never arrived.

She must decide what to tell her son. She knows that if she instructed him to destroy the envelope upon her eventual death, he would do it. Of this, she has no doubt. Mirek would never know that his father did not die immediately after he was born and lived almost fifty years in Israel. He would not learn he is not alone, that he has a half sister, Berta Drůzová, who lives with her husband and two children in Haifa and spells her name without the circle above the *u* and without the Czech suffix *–ová*.

Kiss Mirek for me. At the end of every letter for fifty years, always the same: Kiss Mirek. She owes him hundreds of kisses.

At the time, her whole life revolved around the child. She didn't sleep; she was nervous all the time, inundated with daily cares, which seemed overwhelming only because they were new. Milan gradually distanced himself from her and closed himself off. He refused to take the new situation into consideration, as if he didn't understand she couldn't always be at his beck and call like before. She did not have the right to judge him. But he judged and condemned her and then disappeared. He didn't give her the least opportunity to defend herself. And she would have gone anywhere with him. Done anything. He doubted her and thereby betrayed her. How dare he! Surreptitiously, behind her back, as if he were alone on the planet!

And even though she explained his departure to herself a million times and a million times understood him in her mind, she would not forgive him.

But perhaps she can let Mirek to do it for her. She finally makes up her mind, with difficulty.

After her death.

After all, she does not have to be there to answer his questions. No, she does not.

What will she say to her son tomorrow? She'll simply not ask him to destroy the letters. She will tell him nothing at all.

Kristýna can feel the relief. She has to thank Father Dominik; he was right: A woman cannot remain alone with such things. She should give him a painting when she gets out of here.

She rolls over on her right side with a soft moan and reaches for the plastic tray. She places the pills in her mouth, washes them down with water, and turns out the lamp.

A clean line moves through her mind when she closes her eyes—a light encountering another light halfway. A simple curve, a white horizon, air, air and lightness. The curve is breathing, sinking beyond the horizon. Snow or a desert, swaying, the curve is swaying. The light encounters the light precisely halfway.

When she pulls the curtains back from the hospital window, she sees a desert. In the dim light of dawn, it resembles a sea of snow etched with skeletons of fruit trees. White and black. Ahura Mazda and Angra Mainyu. Theodor Noor is now in Palestine, and Berta sees a definite internal logic to this. Where else could he end up? Where else but in the desert do good and evil culminate? Perhaps in prison, she thinks.

At one time, she genuinely worshiped Theodor Noor. Robert Meinlich less so. He did not succeed in setting alight the shabby cloth of Marxism with his mystic flame. Meinlich the man showed through too much. Whereas earlier, he was a god.

Or perhaps at a certain point, she lost the ability to devote herself to anyone completely.

She devoted herself to her child, whose movements she had already started to feel. All the worse.

The sun will come up in a moment above the snow-covered plain.

The woman without a head—which they had built from freshly fallen snow on the way from school at the end of November 1918—was pregnant, recalls Berta. Pregnant and without a head.

At the time, Rudi was already dead.

Rudi, who informed her even before their first kiss, Love is a catastrophe. I can feel it rolling over me and I dread it. And you?

I don't, said Berta. She was compelled to be older and braver because he expected it of her. She stimulated him, supplied him patiently with courage, until he found his way into her. By the sharp pain, she knew he was in her, but she did not feel any pleasure. Not even the second time. Perhaps the third time it would be better, she thought, but she and Rudi never made it that far.

A pregnant woman without a head.

An empty woman. Her new emptiness is emptier than ever before. The difference consists of five months. For five months, she saw herself as a planted garden; she soared above herself and marveled at how many nice and cozy corners emerged, how many pleasant glades she could relax in, what a pleasant, fragrant warm breeze.

A woman desert.

My love, cries Berta, and doesn't have in mind Rudi or Milan, or even Max.

She's walking with her father to the market. Long, long ago. She is little and her father leans on her as on a milestone. She bears his weight proudly. It is November; the bare tree-tops swarm with crows; the blackbirds restlessly lounge on the branches like poisonous fruit. The sky is almost a violet-gray and you can feel snow in the air. It's cabbage season. From far and wide, farmers have come to the market bearing bushels of cabbages. They pour them out of burlap bags right on the ground. Piles and piles of light green cabbage shimmer beneath the dark, low sky. The clean and shiny heads stripped of their outer leaves seem chilly as they touch the cold stones and freezing mud.

Upon returning home, she paints a picture. She paints without thinking, led only by the powerful impression. When the picture is finished, it's as if she's relieved, free once again. The November afternoon, crows, the macabre beauty of the light green abundance against the dark sky are now transfixed on a piece of paper, forever. Perhaps others do not see it, but Berta does.

She has discovered a rare secret. Now nothing will ever torment her again. All she has to do is paint it. Conjure it up on paper. The secret makes her feel significant and more self-confident, less abandoned, almost happy.

Death cannot be painted. Only survived.

CHAPTER 11

Jerusalem

23 April 2002, Prague
Dear Aaron,

Do you still remember me? It's already been nearly a year. How are you? What have you been doing? Do you have a lot of work? I'm still in school; it seems there's no end to it. I'm still not married either (ha-ha-ha).

We sent Viki the funeral notice, but I don't know if you are still in contact with her and Noah and whether they had a chance to tell you that my grandmother passed away.

It was really unexpected and I still can't get used to the fact that she's not here. Even though it's been almost five months. I still miss her a lot. But you certainly remember her. She was simply an extraordinary individual. She left behind her a void, if you know what I mean. With her, there was no end of surprises. Not even after her death. Do you know what happened?

After she died, we discovered an envelope of letters in her bookcase. Here we learned that my grandfather, my father's father, was Milan Drůza, the Milan Drůza who lived with Berta Altmann before she died in Auschwitz. He survived the concentration camp but did not die in

1948, as Grandmother had always claimed. He fled that year to Israel! There he got married again, had a child, and died only recently. And he kept up a correspondence with my grandmother the whole time, and Father knew nothing about it!

Isn't that insane? We had no idea there were Jews in our family. We didn't know anything. I cannot understand at all how Grandmother managed to hide it or why she did. Father broke down when he found out; he's terribly angry at my grandmother. He says she had no right to keep his father a secret from him, and that it's just another example of how little she cared for him.

From the letters, we also learned that we have relatives in Israel, an aunt named Berta and her two children. She's a graphic artist and lives in Haifa. We found her address, and Father immediately got in touch with her. They agreed we would visit them as soon as possible. I'm going, too.

So, we're arriving in two weeks. I wanted to write you earlier about it, but I didn't know the precise date. Things always kept changing. But now we have the plane tickets and everything is planned. From the twentieth to the twenty-third of May, in exactly a month, we'll be in Jerusalem—sleeping at our aunt's friends'.

So perhaps we could see each other!

I know you have a lot of work and maybe you won't even be there. But if you will, I'd really like to see you. Over the past year, I've often thought about you.

Please write back soon so I'll know one way or another, and forgive me for ambushing you like this.

Very much looking forward to seeing you.

Milena

Aaron straightens himself up behind the wheel and with one hand massages his aching shoulder muscles. He read recently in some magazine that people who for a period of time play a role that does not correspond to their internal makeup often cramp up. That could be an explanation. That is, if he's not satisfied with the explanation that he's old and his neck hurts from lugging a camera around.

The light turns green, but only a couple of cars make it through the intersection before they stop again. He looks at his watch. Ten to three. He can still make it in time. That is, if in the end he doesn't decide not to go meet Milena.

He tries to think it over again, calmly. A year has gone by and that which he somewhat rashly told himself was love has somewhat lost its edge. He no longer suffers from waves of acute nostalgia. His relationship with Lu keeps getting worse, but that has nothing to do with it, and he'll have to deal with it eventually anyway. He goes through the intersection and turns left. A little farther on, he enters a one-way street, at the end of which is the café where he told Milena to meet him. It's easy to find, he had written. It's called the Tower of David and is the only café on this side of the street where you can sit outside.

If only he'd said he wouldn't be in Jerusalem between the twentieth and the twentieth-third of May. She herself had offered him this way out.

Meeting up for coffee! At best, it will be awkward. Both of them will be disappointed and not know what to say. And at worst, thinks Aaron, he'll fall in love with her again. Again he'll flutter about, neglect his work, argue with Lu, and drink. What's the point of seeing each other if there's no way they can be together? If only he were at least ten years younger. Then things would be different! He could go to another country and give it a try. But now he can't start all over! He's got all his contacts here, his social network, an apartment that he's not even had time to arrange. And a son. Because of Viktor, he can no longer budge. But maybe she could move here. She could finish school, find work. It would be a lot easier for her. Aaron catches himself sketching out the future. How ridiculous! What could she possibly do here? Who would come to this country if they didn't have to? Certainly not Milena from Prague, who once confided to him that even pictures on her walls make her feel confined, and that's why she leaves them bare. Milena, who always carries her toothbrush around with her because she never knows where the day will end. Aaron has to laugh at the image. And where, in fact, does he get off hoping she feels something for him? She hasn't written him for an entire year and must have known he was waiting, after what happened between them in Prague. Now she wants to see him only because she doesn't know anyone else in Jerusalem. It's silly to expect anything more. She's young, she's got her own life, and she definitely has a boyfriend. It would be a miracle if she didn't. Her e-mail sounded neutral. Neither excited nor eager, and definitely not amorous. And that's what their meeting will be like. Friends—or rather, acquaintances. If he decides to go, that is.

Does he need to?

Aaron's heart starts pounding, thrashing about in the grip of his rib cage. He parks the car, slides over to the passenger seat, and pulls down the sun visor. In the mirror fixed to the other side, he examines his dark face with its receding hairline and wrinkle-lined eyes, alarmed and uncertain, which remind him of his son's brown eyes. He is looking in the mirror for a cue, a hint of an answer to his question: Meet with Milena or not? Perhaps his face knows the answer, but he is unable to decipher it. He heaves a sigh, steps out of the car, locks it, and with the heavy step of a condemned man sets out toward the café.

Light, untidily tied hair spreading down her back.

He doesn't have to see any more. He summons up the girl clearly, the way she sits, the way she smokes, they way she passes her finger over her upper lip. He recalls the touch of that lip, her soft and warm skin, all of that pulsating, moist being he once pressed to himself.

Aaron steps toward her and thinks it is time to make some changes.

Endnotes

1.

MÉLISANDE: Ah! He's behind a tree!

PELLÉAS: Who?

MÉLISANDE: Goulaud!

PELLÉAS: Goulaud? Where? I see nothing.

MÉLISANDE: There . . . at the end of our shadows.

PELLÉAS: Yes, yes; I can see him . . . Don't turn away too
    suddenly.

MÉLISANDE: He's got his sword . . .

PELLÉAS: I haven't got mine here . . .

MÉLISANDE: He saw, I know he saw us kissing . . .

PELLÉAS: He doesn't know that we've seen him . . . Don't
    move an inch; don't turn your head or he might rush out.
    He's watching us . . . He's standing there without moving.
    You go, now go, go at once, this way . . . I'll wait for him
    . . . I'll keep him off . . .

MÉLISANDE: No, no!

PELLÉAS: Quickly, quickly!

MÉLISANDE: No!

PELLÉAS: He saw it all! He'll kill us both!

MÉLISANDE: Let him! Let him!

PELLÉAS: Here he comes!

MÉLISANDE: Let him!

PELLÉAS: Your lips! Your lips!

MÉLISANDE: Yes! . . . Yes! . . . Yes!

PELLÉAS: Oh! Oh! All the stars of heaven are falling!

MÉLISANDE: On me as well! On me as well!

PELLÉAS: Again, yes, again! Be mine!

MÉLISANDE: I'm all yours! all yours! all yours!

PELLÉAS: . . . Give me, give me . . .

(Goulaud falls upon them, sword in hand.)

MÉLISANDE: Oh! Oh! I have no more courage! I have no more
courage! . . . Ah!

[trans. Hugh Macdonald in *Pelléas & Mélisande, Claude
Debussy,* ed. John Nicholas (London, NY: Riverrun Press,
1982) 83–84.]

2.

Sleep and death, the dusky eagles
Nightlong rush about my head:
Icy tides of eternity would drown
Man's golden image. On jagged reefs
His purple body
Lies shattered.
And the dark echoes
Sound over the sea
Sister of stormy sadness
Behold the lonely sunken skiff
'Neath starry skies,
The silent face of night.

3.
I often think they have only just gone out,
soon they will come back home.
The day is fine, don't be alarmed,
They have just gone for a long walk.

Indeed, they've just gone out,
and now they are making their way home.
Don't be dismayed, the day is fine,
they've simply made a journey to yonder heights.

They have just gone out ahead of us,
and will no longer be coming home.
We go to meet them on yonder heights
In the sunlight, the day is fine
On yonder heights.

BELLEVUE LITERARY PRESS has been publishing
prize-winning books since 2007 and is the first and only
nonprofit press dedicated to literary fiction and nonfiction
at the intersection of the arts and sciences. We believe
that science and literature are natural companions for
understanding the human experience. Our ultimate goal is
to promote science literacy in unaccustomed ways and
offer new tools for thinking about our world.
To support our press and its mission, and for our full
catalogue of published titles, please visit us at blpress.org.

BELLEVUE LITERARY PRESS
New York